Heritage Reclaimed

Caroline's Heritage Series

Book Two:
HERITAGE RECLAIMED

Gaile Thulson

Cup of Water Publishing

HERITAGE RECLAIMED
Copyright © 2017 by Gaile Thulson

All Rights Reserved.
No part of this book may be reproduced, scanned, or distributed in any printed or electronic form without permission.

All people, places, and events of this book are entirely fictional. Any resemblance to real people, places, or events is coincidental. Trademarks mentioned in the text are the property of their respective owners. No endorsement or association is implied by their use.

Scriptures taken from the *Holy Bible, New International Version®, NIV®.* Copyright © 1973, 1978, 1984, 2011 by Biblica, Inc.™ Used by permission of Zondervan. All rights reserved worldwide. www.zondervan.com The "NIV" and "New International Version" are trademarks registered in the United States Patent and Trademark Office by Biblica, Inc.™

Cover design © 2017 by Cup of Water Publishing, LLC

ISBN 978-0-9973279-3-9 (Hardcover)
ISBN 978-0-9973279-4-6 (Paperback)
ISBN 978-0-9973279-5-3 (eBook)

To my husband Mark
whose love and faithfulness
made these books possible

Caroline's Heritage Series

Book One: Heritage Restored
Book Two: Heritage Reclaimed

*Your statutes are my heritage forever;
they are the joy of my heart.*

Psalm 119:111

Heritage Reclaimed

CHAPTER ONE

"Stopped for cookie decorations. I'll be there in ten minutes." Caroline Engbert picked up her phone to read Jo's text. Her friend Jo was driving from her home in another suburb, but it would only take Caroline a minute to run next door to Jo's grandparents' house for lunch and an afternoon of Christmas baking. Caroline headed to the elegant powder room on the main floor of the house she had inherited from her own grandparents, ran a brush through her hair, and then grabbed her jacket from the front coat closet. She jogged across the broad cul-de-sac with her usual level of energy and a smile on her face.

"Caroline, it's so good to see you," said Jo's grandmother, Martha Lockwood, giving her a hug. "How are you feeling?"

"Great! Thanks to Jo! She'll be here in a minute."

Only a week before, Jo had helped Caroline recover from a bout with the flu. Jo had also helped Caroline pray and receive Christ into her heart and life.

"I'm glad Jo could help. She *is* my granddaughter, and I'm proud of her, but I'm more proud that she walks with the Lord," said Martha with a smile, wanting to give thanks to God. "I'm sure the Holy Spirit was prompting her to go looking for you that day."

"Yes. I know," Caroline answered, understanding Martha's desire to make sure God got the credit. "God sent her in answer to my prayers."

"Isn't it wonderful that God brought such good out of it all? He's the only one who knew you were ready to give your life to him. We're so happy for you, Caroline! Your grandmother must be rejoicing that God has heard her prayers after all these years."

"Yes, I think God was answering all along. It just took me a while to figure out that it was him."

Lunch was a happy occasion. No one wished to be anywhere else or with anyone else, and no one could think of a better reason to celebrate than Caroline's salvation. Not only were Jo and Caroline good friends, Jo's grandparents had been next door neighbors and friends to Caroline's grandparents long before Caroline's birth, and long after as well. Though the Lockwoods now knew that Caroline had come home to live in her grandparents' house after growing up in foster homes because her parents had died when she was young, they didn't know the whole story of her family. They didn't know all that God had done. At least, she didn't think so.

"It's just too bad you couldn't come to live with your grandparents when they were still living," said Jo's grandfather, John Lockwood, looking down at his coffee cup and shaking his head. Meaning to complement Caroline, he continued, "Especially those last few years when Jack was gone. Emily would have been so happy to know you."

"Well, that's God's business. Caroline's and God's," Martha said gently.

Jo smiled gentle encouragement at Caroline while Caroline thought with regret, as she did every day, what little consolation she would have had to offer her Grandmother Emily at that time in her life. Instead of caring for her own grandmother in her last years, God had placed Caroline in her last foster home where she had ended up caring for an elderly invalid and his wife. Instead of causing her grandmother more grief in her grief-filled life, Caroline had learned she must live out at least some small degree of patience and compassion even if it was not returned. It was there, in her final foster home, that her hunger for her real family had gradually grown to an intensity she could no longer ignore. She was beginning to realize that God had used that time to prepare her to come searching for her roots within the walls of her grandparents' home.

Caroline deeply regretted not knowing her grandmother before her death, but she was grateful for the journals her grandmother had left behind. Those journals revealed her grandmother's heart and a great love for God and for her wayward family. It was reading her grandmother's journals that had taught her that God was real and that he answered prayer.

She wondered how well the Lockwoods had really known her grandparents, Jack and Emily Hampden. How much of their story had the Lockwoods known as it actually unfolded? She remembered that their daughter Claire, Jo's mother, had once said that the few years of age difference had resulted in her not knowing the Hampdens as they grew up next door. Caroline's mother and Uncle Brad had attended private schools rather than the schools the Lockwood children attended. Caroline knew from her grandmother's journals that her mother and uncle had also been involved with summer activities in private swim clubs and a country club, so they had not spent their summers hanging out at the lake with their neighbors. Grandfather Jack Hampden's desire to give his children the best had deprived them of many things, including a deep relationship with the godly Lockwood family next door.

Caroline's grandmother had tried to take her children to church when they were small, but Caroline's grandfather had discouraged them from continuing. Caroline smiled to think that she claimed her grandmother's church as her own now, thanks to the Lockwoods' hospitality and persistent invitations. There were so many ways in which God was answering her grandmother's prayers!

Did the Lockwoods know Caroline's mother's story, the story that had shaped Caroline's life so drastically? Caroline didn't want everyone to know her family stories, but she resolved on the spur of the moment to be completely honest with these friends of her grandparents who were becoming so precious to Caroline. The Lockwoods had insisted on becoming her surrogate grandparents, and they deserved to know the whole story. She placed the Christmas cookie she had decided to sample back on her plate.

"I want you to know what happened," she said quietly.

"You don't have to tell us anything, dear," said Martha.

"No. I want you to know. Jo knows." Caroline took a deep breath. "Where should I start?"

Her audience waited patiently.

"I came here looking for answers to that very question. I wanted to know why I hadn't known my grandparents. I didn't even know my grandparents were alive all that time. I didn't know they were looking for me."

John Lockwood frowned and stared into his coffee, deeply shocked, but didn't comment. In all of their conversations with Caroline, this had never before been revealed.

Caroline continued, "I had some vague memories of them from my first few years of life. I came here to find out why they had never claimed me. Why they didn't want me. Why they had never offered me a home."

John stirred restlessly, his frown deepening, but Martha laid a quieting hand on his arm.

"I know more of the truth now. I know they did want me." Caroline smiled weakly at John. "My mother died when I was four. I only knew she had died in a car accident. My father died when I was five. According to the records I later gained access to, he died rather suddenly of cancer. I was put into foster homes and didn't know I had any living relatives until last year when the lawyers contacted me, explaining that my grandmother had recently died and left me everything. I was in shock! I didn't know what to do. Everyone I asked recommended selling the house. To most people, the money it represented was more valuable than a house in another state, a house I knew nothing about. So, I asked the lawyers to work with me to put it into shape for prospective buyers.

"I was so confused. I thought my grandparents must not have loved me, because they hadn't made any effort to contact me the whole time I was growing up. I kept wondering why they would leave everything to me. It was so amazing! I knew they knew about me, because I thought I had memories of being with them. I supposed there wasn't anyone else, so the house came to me as the closest relative. But when I got the actual papers from the lawyers, it was clear that my grandparents had named me by name as their heir. Grandmother Emily had made sure that I would be found and notified of her death." Caroline paused for a sip of water.

"I was hurt and angry at my parents, and my grandparents, and especially at God." She fought back the tears that threatened to interrupt. "The last few years have been difficult. The Axels, the foster couple I lived with during my last years of high school and a year at the community college, weren't well. They let me stay because they needed help. Then Mr. Axel died, and Mrs. Axel sort of checked out. I had run their finances and medical treatments for the last couple of years, so I helped her sort things out. She sold everything and went to live with her sister. I knew I wanted to finish college, but other than that I was really struggling with what to do next. I decided to come and try to find out what had happened. I wanted to know if my memories of having a family were real."

"You poor dear," murmured Martha, squeezing Caroline's hand.

Her sympathy caused tears to spill from Caroline's eyes. She swallowed hard and dabbed her eyes with the tissue Jo provided.

"I found my grandmother's journals in her study. She left them for me so I would know that she and Grandpa loved me. It was great to read about my mother and my uncle as children growing up here. But you know my grandfather wasn't a Christian. He had a drinking problem. My uncle Brad got into alcohol and drugs. From what I read in

7

Grandmother's journals, I think it nearly destroyed him more than once, but he did accept Christ the day before he died."

Martha nodded. "I remember. Your grandmother came over and told me. She sat at this table and we cried together. It was so hard for her to lose him, but when she finally got word that he had become a Christian, it made it so much easier for her. She was so thankful that she would see him again in heaven."

"Reading how God had answered Grandma's prayers for Uncle Brad before he died was my first hint that God did care." Caroline paused. "Did you know about the drug and alcohol addictions in my family back then?" she asked.

"We knew Jack had a drinking problem, but most people didn't. He hid it well," John Lockwood said.

"I prayed with your Grandmother Emily sometimes when things were particularly difficult for her," Martha said, "but I didn't know anything about drugs."

"Uncle Brad had a difficult time growing up. He turned to drugs and alcohol when he was very young. Then my mom started dabbling in drugs. When she met my dad and ran away with him, I guess it was pretty awful for Grandma to be the only one praying. You can tell from what she wrote in her journals that she loved them all so much. Anyway, when I was born, my mom finally brought me here when I was two months old, to show to her parents. I learned things from Grandmother's journals about my dad's life that made me ashamed. I'm thankful my mom was able to stay away from alcohol and drugs when she was expecting me. She wanted me to be healthy, but after I was born, I guess it got pretty bad. My dad was a heavy drug user and an alcoholic. He didn't want Mom and me to be here at all, so we could only come when Mom could sneak away. But those are the times I remember being happy. Those are the memories that brought me back here looking for answers."

"I remember when you were little, Caroline. Back then, your grandmother kept many of her family troubles to herself. I suspected, but I didn't know all of this. But I *can* tell you this: she just lived for your visits!" Martha said, clasping Caroline's hand.

"I remember them as such happy times." Caroline smiled through her tears. "But then, I read in Grandmother's journal that my grandfather had been driving when my mom was killed in the accident. Grandmother never really said it, but I think she suspected my grandfather had been drinking."

"We wondered, too," John said. "He had such a horrible time with his guilt."

"I was so shocked I didn't want to read any more. I'm afraid I had idealized my parents and grandparents. I thought if they had only lived, my life would have been so much better. I always thought God must not be real, or he must not care about people, because he let my parents die so young. I know my mom did accept the Lord. She prayed with

Grandmother the day before the accident, but I was so upset by what I read in Grandmother's journals, I didn't want anything to do with God."

"What changed that?" asked Martha.

"I guess it was my grandmother's prayers. She prayed that I would grow up safe from the heritage of addiction in our family. I learned that God had ultimately answered her prayers for my uncle, and my mom, and even my Grandfather, but I didn't want to give God the credit for my safety. He had made me grow up in foster homes! I was still angry and confused. I didn't want to go with Jo to the mission two weeks ago. I was so humiliated by what I'd learned about my family. I sat there the whole time, thinking I could be homeless or addicted. It could so easily be me sitting out there!"

"I'm sorry, Caroline," murmured Jo.

"But it's okay! God used the experience at the mission to show me that he loved me. He loved all of the people at the mission! He loved my family, and he loved me!"

"We're all sinners," said John.

"Yes," said Martha, "we're all sinners in God's eyes, but his mercy is big enough to forgive any of us."

"I finally figured that out," admitted Caroline with a trace of a smile. "And then I got sick. Thanks for looking out for me! I can see all of it helped me understand I needed to be forgiven. I needed Jesus.

After I prayed with Jo and then later when she'd gone home, I finished reading my grandmother's last journal. That's when I learned that my dad took me away after the accident and got a restraining order against my grandparents."

"Oh my goodness! They must have been mortified! They never told us!" exclaimed Martha. "I wish we'd known half of what they were going through! Your grandmother told me later that they were trying to find you but couldn't."

"Yes, they tried. But I guess I found the answer to my biggest question," Caroline said. "It turns out, they never knew about my father's death. They assumed he would remarry. They weren't informed of his death, and they didn't know I'd been placed in foster homes. They never knew!"

"I was surprised when you first came by yourself. Then Jo said you'd grown up in foster homes. I just couldn't understand that! If you only knew how much your grandparents wanted you!" exclaimed Martha.

"But that's how God answered all of my grandmother's prayers for me. She asked God to let me grow up free of addictions, no matter what it took to make it happen. That's the reason I grew up apart from the heritage I wanted so badly. Now I know that the things God denied me could have destroyed me."

"It's because he loved you that you were denied your family all those years," observed Jo.

11

"Yes. I finally know."

"Well, I'll be," said John.

"Caroline, I'm so sorry we didn't know more of what your grandparents went through. And so sorry your life was like that," Martha said.

"It was hard, but it's so good now," Caroline acknowledged, smiling through her tears.

"Grandpa, could we pray for Caroline?" Jo asked.

"Why sure! Let's do that right now."

Jo and her grandmother clasped Caroline's hands as John began.

"Lord, we want to thank you for Caroline and for what you've done in her life. Thank you for Emily and Jack, and for bringing their granddaughter Caroline home after all of these years."

Martha continued, "Help us to be good neighbors and grandparents to Caroline, Lord. Thank you so much for bringing her here. Thank you for answering Emily's prayers. Thank you for keeping Caroline safe. Thank you most of all for your salvation. Thank you that we will see Emily and Jack in heaven. Thank you that we'll see their children in heaven, and thank you for bringing Caroline to you, Jesus."

"Lord Jesus, would you please heal Caroline's heart?" Jo prayed. "We ask that you would continually work your miracle of love and healing in her life. Thank you for restoring all that she has lost of her heritage, with your own all-sufficient presence and your goodness. Help her to reclaim the spiritual heritage her grandmother provided for her. Help her to know the depth of your love for her. Provide for her needs. Draw her close to you and help her to walk with you each day. Thank you for her grandmother's prayers and for her journals. Thank you for bringing Caroline here to find out what happened and to find you."

"Thank you for hearing our prayers. In Christ's name, Amen," John concluded.

Caroline could only sit and let the tears flow. "Thank you," she managed to say.

Martha got up to give her a hug. "The past is past, but God can still heal it. Let's have some fun while we're thanking God for the here and now. What he has done is worth celebrating! John, would you put on some Christmas carols for us? I think it's time to decorate Christmas cookies!"

"Which ones are we making today?" asked Jo.

"The recipe's on the counter, so you and Caroline go ahead and get started while I clean up and get organized. It's the sugar cookies today."

"I've done this every Christmas with Grandma," Jo explained to Caroline. "These are the fun ones because we get to cut out different shapes, and the frosting's so good! Here are the cookie cutters. We do the star shape for the Bethlehem star. Here's the camel the wise men came on.

Well, at least they probably came on camels. Here are Mary and Joseph kneeling. Grandpa made those two cookie cutters. Where did you get the others, Grandma?"

"Oh, I think they were your great-grandmother's. We had them when I was a little girl. We used them every Christmas. Never missed a year. Ever since I can remember!" Martha gave the girls a hug, one in each arm, as they stood reading the recipe. "I'm so glad you're here to help!" She pushed aside thoughts of future years with her granddaughter now a senior in college and potentially leaving the area before long. How had Jo grown up so quickly? The years seemed to fly by, but she was grateful. How many grandmothers got to enjoy a granddaughter in their life for this long? She refused to worry about how many more years Jo would be cutting out Christmas cookies in her kitchen! That was God's business. She knew Jo was willing to go anywhere God wanted her, and if God wanted Jo on the mission field, as Jo planned, then that would be better than making cookies with her grandmother.

"How many do we need?" Jo asked.

"I think just double the recipe. I have some cookies already done. The chocolate drops and snickerdoodles are already in the freezer. Maybe Monday we can make the Rice Krispie bars with chocolate frosting and the peanut butter cookies with the Hershey Kiss in the middle."

"Okay. What about the pecan snowballs?"

"Oh, I forgot! I have the ingredients, I think. So we'll see how far we get today."

Caroline got ready to measure and mix ingredients as Jo brought them to her.

"I'll go ahead and cream the butter and confectioners' sugar together first," Caroline said, looking the recipe over. "Then it looks like we could add all of the other ingredients and the flour last. Is that all right?"

"Yup! That's good! We always combine all of the wet ingredients first, then add everything else, and the flour last," Jo explained. "It saves a lot of time and mess."

"I do that too," Caroline assented. It was a useful thing one of her foster mothers had explained to her. It didn't work with more complex recipes, but it certainly made sense for many of the straightforward ones. In this case, she needed to mix the butter and sugar together, then the eggs and other ingredients to ensure the batter had the necessary creamy, voluminous base. After that, it was easy to add the flavorings and other ingredients to the bowl before adding the flour. That way, the seasonings were evenly distributed in the same bowl, instead of dirtying another bowl with all of the dry ingredients sifted together. Caroline was glad she wouldn't have to slavishly follow the directions. She had learned that every family had their own way of doing things, and sometimes they weren't open to suggestions from outsiders, no matter how much sense it made. She didn't mind at all

15

that Jo and her grandmother had their list of Christmas cookies that they made every year. In fact, she was glad to participate and claim their traditions as her own. It was almost like being part of the family she had missed out on.

"Go easy on the flour," Jo recommended. "We have to use a lot when we roll it out, so it doesn't stick. So we don't add all of the flour at first. Maybe, hold back at least a half cup."

"Will do," Caroline assured her. "Do you give out your recipes, or are they family secrets?" she asked Martha.

"Oh, there's nothing secret about my recipes," laughed Martha.

"I'd love to have some of your Christmas cookie recipes." Caroline had a collection of her favorite recipes from a variety of the families she had lived with, and now she had the recipes her grandmother had left in her own kitchen next door. She was enjoying trying different ones, beginning with the recipe cards that were in the worst shape, obviously her grandmother's favorites.

"I'll get you a pen and some cards. I'm flattered that you want them!" Martha said.

Martha found the recipes for the cookies that had already been made, and Caroline copied those while Jo began rolling out the sugar cookie dough.

"This is a nice soft dough," Caroline commented when she rejoined the process.

"You saw how sticky it was at first. We don't refrigerate

it before rolling it out. I suppose that's why it takes so much flour to keep it from sticking, but it's easier to roll out when it's soft, and there's no delay. We can bake them right away."

Caroline helped as they filled cookie sheets with cutouts, put them in the oven, and filled more cookie sheets to take the place of the ones already in the oven. After a surprisingly short time, they pulled the cookies out of the oven.

"We like them soft. It's easy to overbake these," Jo explained, handing Caroline a broken cookie fresh from the oven.

"Wow! I love the almond flavor," Caroline commented. "Mmmm... so soft and warm."

"They're even better with the frosting. It has almond extract, too. If we could only figure out how to have frosting on a warm cookie straight from the oven, now that would be the perfect cookie! The frosting tends to melt if the cookies are too warm."

Caroline relaxed into the warm sharing of the Lockwood family traditions. The kitchen was filled with heavenly smells as she and Jo quickly stacked the cutout sugar cookies with waxed paper between layers, sealed them inside clean plastic ice cream buckets, and placed them in Martha's extra freezer. As the sugar cookies chilled in the freezer, they started on their next assignment.

"I like the crunch of the pecans in these," said Caroline, already familiar with them.

When the snowballs were baked and rolled in confectioners' sugar, they were layered into more buckets, sealed, and placed in the freezer.

"That's a great way to store cookies until you want them," Caroline observed.

"Stale cookies are the worst, aren't they? I'm afraid Grandpa likes his ice cream," Jo whispered. "Grandma always has plenty of these plastic ice cream buckets."

Caroline laughed.

"What do you think, Grams? Do we have time to frost the sugar cookies now?" Jo asked.

"You girls may have better things to do."

"Nope, Grandma. I'm staying until they're done," said Jo. "You don't have to stay, Caroline, if you have other things you need to do."

"No, I'd like to stay and help so I get the frosting right when I make them on my own."

"Oh, good!" exclaimed Jo. "I'm glad! They do take a while to frost if we want them to look really professional. We can use all the help we can get."

Caroline's artistic flair came to the front as they piped dark green, a lighter green, white, and red frosting and then used candy silver balls, red hots, and sprinkles to decorate the fragrant cookies. The scent of almond, the sound of traditional Christmas carols, and the pleasant tasks with these people she had already learned to love entered Caroline's soul to do some of the healing Jo had prayed for right there in Martha Lockwood's cozy family kitchen. When they were finished, several buckets filled with perfectly frosted cookies went back into the freezer to await Christmas day. The "rejects" were placed on a plate for the Lockwoods, but Martha insisted on sending home a few of the best with each of the girls.

Caroline trotted home across the cul-de-sac and carefully placed her cookies in the freezer for later. Christmas carols were soon ringing through her house, helping Caroline to prolong the happiness of sharing Christmas preparations with Jo and her grandparents. She had been invited to spend Christmas day at Jo's family home and looked forward to the experience. She was sure Jo's brother Peter would be there. She told herself she merely wanted to thank him for helping to set up her computer equipment when she had first arrived; but the one day they'd spent together had grown larger in importance over the months, and she was anxious to see if he measured up to her memories. She remembered every part of that day, and very nearly every word they had exchanged.

CHAPTER TWO

The days leading up to Christmas were busy ones for Caroline. She spent significant amounts of time reading her grandmother's Bible, soaking up the daily study in the Gospel of John, and finding other interesting parts of the Bible to read as well. She loved the Psalms, especially when Jo explained that many were written out of the stress of King David's life as prophetic statements of Christ's future sufferings. It seemed beyond understanding that a psalm could meet her daily needs on such a personal level with God, as well as reflecting the circumstances of an ancient king's life and, especially, Christ's suffering during his life on earth. Jo had sketched out a simple timeline of important people in the Bible so Caroline could easily see where they fit into major events in God's schedule. King David had lived roughly a thousand years before Jesus, and it was Jesus who was the promised descendant of David. Jesus was the promised Messiah. It was Jesus who would rule as king forever. Caroline marveled at how amazing God was and how amazing his Word was!

Each day now became a gift from God, a cherished, private, almost holy time of healing. There was incredible peace in having long private days of making her own choices, of directing her own life in ways she believed would please God, and of thankfully appreciating the luxurious setting of her grandparents' home.

She relished having time to play her grandmother's grand piano and to spruce up her rusty technique with no one listening. And no one competing for the piano! Since she had begun piano lessons at an early age, each foster home had tried to continue to provide them, with the result that her teachers and instruction had been widely varied, and interrupted with every move. While this had not been the best situation to turn her into a virtuoso, it had given her a base on which to build some knowledge of music theory and a deep appreciation for music. Her best high school experiences had been the choirs and musicals in which she had participated. Now, she had a new interest in Christian music. It seemed to speak to her so deeply. She loved playing her grandmother's hymns and was able to find music for some of the contemporary Christian songs that the worship team at church used. Praise for the Lord seemed to flow out of her grateful heart on a daily basis.

With no college classes going on, Caroline spent extra time working on her senior project but was more and more caught up in exploring the house she now called home.

Though school would not resume for nearly a month, she had decided to decorate sparingly this year. She did not want to spend her limited time putting it all away again. Maybe next year she'd have a little more time. Hopefully, next year she wouldn't be sick with Christmas coming on, and by then she would have a better idea of how she wanted to decorate a house that still seemed new to her.

She did spend time one day going through a few of her grandparents' Christmas boxes stored in the basement and choosing a few things that pleased her to display in strategic places around the main floor of the house. Putting up one of the smallest imitation trees on an entryway table helped her to be cheerful, and it made it seem more like Christmas. One discovery made her grateful that her grandmother had taken such good care of the things that were important to her. Caroline carefully carried the entire box up to the kitchen to examine its contents. What a find! Many of the decorations looked like antiques, but it was the ones that she knew her grandmother had valued the most that intrigued her. They were stored with notes regarding their family history, telling who had gifted them to her or who had made them. She took the handmade decorations produced by her mother and Uncle Brad up to her room because they seemed so precious. Wanting to have them near to her, where she could see them and handle them at the end of each day, she examined the childish craftsmanship and signatures on the back over and

23

over. It somehow made the people in her family more real.

A generous portion of warm heather tweed in her grandmother's sewing room inspired her to begin work on a jacket and flared skirt to wear with boots. There were several other pieces that she could imagine would help her round out her winter wardrobe. She wanted to take advantage of the free fabric and get as many of them made as she could before school started again. In the meantime, Christmas was rapidly approaching, and she enjoyed window shopping. She found it easy to fantasize about generous purchases for herself and her new friends; so she forced herself to focus on deciding what she would actually give the important people in her life.

Deciding to make good use of Martha Lockwood's and her grandmother's recipes, she delivered a plate of Christmas cookies and candies to the elderly neighbors who lived on the other side of the Lockwoods and to the house next to her on the opposite side from the Lockwoods. Though on the cul-de-sac, their house was some distance from hers, facing the cross street rather than the cul-de-sac, so she and the Lockwoods rarely saw them. She had heard they were a young couple with two children, and it seemed they were constantly on the go with both parents working and the kids in school, sports, and other activities. Cookies in hand, she rang their doorbell, determined to introduce herself. Two dogs added to the wholesome noise when the door opened, and the kids seemed genuinely excited about the colorful plate of goodies. Now that they had exchanged names, she hoped they would wave if they saw her out and about.

※

Caroline woke at her usual early hour. Christmas morning! *Thank you, Jesus! Thank you, Jesus!* What were the words from Psalm 103 that she had read just before falling asleep last night? *Praise the Lord, O my soul; all my inmost being, praise his holy name.* Smiling, she thought how strange it was on a Christmas morning, to be alone in a quiet house! She lay still, listening to the solitude, but felt only God's peace as she reflected back on previous Christmases that had been filled with longing for her own family. Unlike those Christmases Past, she had so much to look forward to now! In spite of the fact that she would never spend Christmas day with her family, her future no longer seemed uncertain or lacking, but full of possibilities. She was more excited about this Christmas day than any she could remember! And on this morning that seemed to her like a first-of-its-kind Christmas morning, she wanted extra time to spend with Jesus while reading her Bible. After all, it was his birthday.

There were no presents to open, but there was a new outfit to wear that had been her early present to herself, and she was looking forward to a special breakfast. The habit of not eating after dinnertime kept her trim and enabled her to enjoy breakfast each morning, but, today, she would splurge with her special apple-filled, cinnamon French toast. Or maybe one of her other favorites. Homemade blueberry waffles? She jumped out of bed, going through a mental to-do list. She had been asked to bring tossed salads for the Berkhardts' late lunch, their official Christmas dinner. Shopping for the ingredients had been fun, and she would try to make them as festive as possible with bright pomegranate seeds and a special homemade dressing.

She still had a few presents to wrap and other jobs to complete before Jo and Peter picked her up for Christmas dinner. There was a great deal to do! So, she sang her way through the morning, looking forward to spending Christmas with the Berkhardts. She hadn't seen Peter since he'd arrived at his parents' home two days before Christmas, but she was excited about the soft wool scarf she had made for him. She'd made one for Jo, too, so it didn't seem too awkward to give it to him. A free book download of their choice for Jo and Peter would round out her gift giving and act as insurance in case the scarves weren't what they would have chosen.

Gift baskets of cheese and crackers for the Lockwoods and Berkhardts, and a generous plate of homemade English toffee to pass around after dinner, made her little cache of gifts large and awkward to carry. When Jo's car pulled up, Caroline didn't have time to wonder what to say. She began piling gifts outside the door, balancing three glass salad bowls since the guest number had recently risen from twelve to thirty-eight! Peter jumped out to help when he saw her dilemma.

"Hi!" she said.

"Merry Christmas! Need some help?"

"Yes! Thank you!"

Jo opened the back so they could deposit everything, and Caroline was soon sitting in the front with Jo. Peter had insisted.

"Thanks for coming all the way over here on Christmas day. I thought I could get by without a car, but maybe I'll have to rethink that," Caroline admitted. She knew both Jo and Peter drove inexpensive but dependable cars that, though used, were still in great shape. Maybe she'd sell those gaudy carnival masks that her grandfather had brought back from Venice so many years ago, before he became a Christian. Both Martha Lockwood and her friend Millie Larson had explained that Grandmother Emily had never liked them, and they were supposedly valuable. "Probably not valuable enough for a car," Caroline thought.

"We can pray about that for you," Jo suggested, referring to Caroline's need for a car.

"Yeah! Thanks! That would be a great idea!" Caroline exclaimed.

"Okay, Lord! Caroline needs a cool car to drive!" said Peter, half in earnest, half in jest.

"Okay, Lord! Caroline needs a dependable car she can afford!" countered Jo, laughing. "Maybe you should tell Peter your news. I haven't told him," Jo said, keeping her eyes on the road and grinning.

"What haven't you told me?" Peter joked, pretending to be offended.

Caroline was glad she couldn't see Peter in the seat behind her. It made it easier to say, "Jo helped me pray. I asked Jesus to come into my heart."

"You don't say! Tell me about it!"

Caroline briefly explained the events leading up to her salvation, eliminating much of the personal family information she had confided to Jo and Peter's grandparents. "I'm thankful Jo came."

"Way to go, Sis. Well, I guess you're my sister now, too, Caroline. I'm glad you're part of God's family."

"Thanks," Caroline managed to say. She was glad to be part of God's family, even Peter's family, but she didn't want to be Peter's sister.

During the awkward silence that followed, Peter was analyzing the words that had popped out of his mouth, wondering if God had brought them together so he could be a big brother to Caroline. He was several years older than she was, and now she was a new believer who needed time and opportunity to develop her faith and knowledge of God. Was that what she needed, a big brother? He wondered if she thought he was *old*. Twenty-six wasn't exactly over the hill! His twenty-seventh birthday loomed closer than he wanted to admit. Maybe she saw him as some kind of stick-in-the-mud bachelor working on a Ph.D. with his nose in the books all the time. He did have to stay focused, but he was still fun. Wasn't he? The years had gone so quickly and he had to admit he was totally absorbed with his degree program and trying to build a future. Why had he never met the right girl? Maybe he had, but he'd been too focused on himself and his career to know. That couldn't be true! He'd asked God to help him hold out for the right one, and he knew his life would have been complicated by any commitments before this point. Was now the right timing? But Caroline was so young! True, she was a believer now, but so new in her faith. He didn't even really know her. What he wanted to do most of all now was spend time with her, lots of time. Did he need to be a big brother to her for now? "Help, Lord!" he cried out silently to his Heavenly Father. "I don't know if I can do that!"

Jo had begun telling Caroline about the additional extended family members coming to Christmas dinner. Jo and Peter's mother was the Lockwoods' daughter, but Jo was explaining that some of their dad's family, the Berkhardt side, were in town unexpectedly and counting on Christmas day with them. "So thanks for making all of that salad!" she said to Caroline.

"No problem! It was fun!"

Dinner was nearly ready when they arrived. Peter and Jo rushed around doing last minute things for their mother, and Caroline tried to help, under Jo's direction. Their father, Bret, managed to get everyone's attention once they were all seated at the tables spread throughout the open floor plan.

"Let's thank God together," he said and the room grew silent as all bowed their heads, from the littlest to the oldest. "God, our Father in Heaven, we are gathered here because of your great kindness in sending your Son to live as a human like us. We celebrate today that day over two thousand years ago when you allowed your Son to be born as a baby here on the earth. Thank you for sending him, not to the rich but to the poor, not to the rulers but to the common people, not to the arrogant and full but to the needy. So today, Lord God, we acknowledge our need for your Son and the salvation you made available through faith in him. We thank you for offering us peace with you when we only deserve your judgment. We thank you, Heavenly Father, for all the blessings available to us through your Son, Jesus. We thank you for your care and protection and ask you to bless this amazing feast you have provided. We ask you to bless each person here and to fill our hearts with your presence and your goodness, and we give you all of the glory. We ask it all in Christ's name. Amen."

Caroline and Jo were seated, according to place cards, with some of the younger Berkhardt cousins. Peter was sitting at the other end of the table with older cousins, one of whom immediately became interested in Caroline.

"Why should I be surprised?" Peter tried to reason with himself. "She's a beautiful young woman and closer to Jon's age than mine." He made himself miserable wondering who Caroline had been hanging around with in his absence. She could have a boyfriend at school or church, for all he knew! Maybe he needed to join the competition before it was too late! He began to wonder how he could get information about Caroline out of Jo without letting his sister know how he felt.

After an introductory exchange, Jon leaned toward Caroline's end of the table and asked her what year she was in school.

"Technically, I'll be a junior this next semester," she replied. "But I'm in a combined undergrad and master's program."

"And smart as all get out!" chimed in Jo. She ignored Caroline's chagrined look and continued. "Gordon Technology Award," Jo explained pointing toward Caroline, seated next to her.

"Well, well," thought Peter. "I'm learning things already. That little fact never came out last fall in our day together setting up her new computer system in her grandfather's study." Beauty and brains, just as he'd suspected.

"How did you know?" Caroline asked Jo.

"Dr. Calton's been bragging about you."

31

"Oh!" Caroline was surprised. It certainly wasn't a secret, but she had been careful not to tell anyone. Sometimes it altered the way people treated her when they found out that she was smart. In foster homes and with school friends, it had often made her life more difficult and lonelier than she'd wanted. She had chosen to spend all of her spare time studying, and very little of it on "girl talk" with foster sisters and their friends. As for guys, she never knew how they were going to react. Surely Peter could not feel intimidated. He was brilliant. But did he date brilliant girls? Whom *did* he date? Did she have any chance with him? She wondered if being a computer science major made her seem less feminine, unaware that there was nothing she could do that would alter her feminine appeal.

She was beginning to understand that her choice to focus single-mindedly on building her future had protected her in many ways, though it had been lonely. Should she have made other choices? She told herself that there was nothing she could do to alter the past. She had to let it go and trust God with her future. After all, he had taken care of her through amazing circumstances. She suspected it would be a gradual revelation from God over the years to come, about the many ways he had watched over her in answer to her grandmother's prayers. Now that she knew God really did care about her and had loved her all those years when she'd been hurting inside, she was grateful.

Caroline listened and watched the Berkhardt family as they enjoyed the exceptional food and each other's company. They seemed so comfortable with one another. There was endless teasing and joking, something she had never been comfortable with herself, but no one here seemed to mind. The teasing never became denigrating or destructive, and she found herself relaxing. These people knew each other so well and were so secure in their acceptance of one another that she felt she could participate with the conversation and fit in, unconcerned about what people thought of her. Even among strangers, she felt safe.

After dinner, everyone enjoyed the impromptu children's acting out of the Christmas story led by Jo's mom who provided simple costumes and directed the action while Jo's dad narrated from the book of Luke; and then the entire group opened gifts in a friendly, chaotic manner. Caroline was surprised by the stack of gifts that came her way. Inexpensive yet thoughtful gifts from the Berkhardts and Lockwoods made her feel accepted and part of the festivities. The Lockwoods' gift turned out to be an elegant, gilt-edged, blank journal. Martha smiled at Caroline when she expressed her thanks. She had anticipated the surprised expression on Caroline's face when she opened the gift and had seen Caroline process the idea that she could, or even should, write her own journal entries to carry on her grandmother's tradition.

Jo reached over to feel the soft journal cover, smiling and adding her surprised approval. Caroline stifled the conflict of emotions she was experiencing, deciding to think about it later, and proceeded to open her other gifts. Jo surprised her with a gift card to the clothing store that had become Caroline's favorite. It wasn't a sizable amount, but generous enough that Caroline could certainly find something worthwhile. After giving Jo a hug, she was able to catch Peter's eye and wave a thank you for an ornate hardcover copy of *Pride and Prejudice*. Peter wrapped her scarf around his neck and waded through the gift wrap that littered the floor.

"Thank you for the scarf. A much-needed protection from the cold," Peter comically told her. "And for the book download."

"Thank you for the book!" she said with a smile.

"I hope you like it. Jo assured me that all young ladies love this book."

"True! Probably true!" Caroline laughed.

"I can return it if you'd rather have an e-book."

"No. I like it! I haven't seen it at my grandparents' house."

"Of course, you may already have it! The danger of purchasing a book all young ladies love."

"I don't think I have a copy! Really! I like it!"

"Do you read much fiction?" he asked.

"I prefer fiction when I have time. It will be great to read it again. This is a good time to enjoy it before school starts again."

"You've read it before?"

"Oh, yes! But that's good! A classic can stand to be read over and over."

"I could exchange it if there's something else you would prefer."

"No. No, it's perfect. Thank you!" She was having trouble convincing him that she was actually quite pleased with the book.

Peter was, at that point, attacked by young relatives armed with wads of gift wrapping, and ultimately tackled to the floor.

"Careful, guys!" he cautioned them as he gently steered them away from gifts stacked on the floor next to the recipients. "How about taking this outside?"

"Take us sledding at the park, Peter!"

"Sledding! That's no fun!" he joked, tickling the one who'd asked. "All right! Let's go! Coming, Caroline? Jo?"

"Where's the park?" Caroline asked.

"It's less than two blocks away. It looks like Mom's getting plenty of help right now. Do you want to go?" Jo asked Caroline.

"Sure!" Caroline hadn't been sledding since middle school. Maybe it would be fun with this crowd.

"Okay! Let's go, kids! But nobody goes without boots and gloves and hats!" Jo warned the younger ones.

"Come, me mateys," Peter growled, hoisting the littlest cousin over his shoulder. "Cap'n says we have to wear boots! So, where are they?" To the delight of the children, Peter attempted to put his giant boots on little Josh's feet and little Josh's boots on his own adult-sized feet. Peter continued to entertain them with comments like, "We'll never make it at this rate, Cap'n!" and "On with the boots, or ye'll be walkin' the plank!"

Jo and Caroline helped everyone find their gloves, scarves, and hats and herded them out the door. The older cousins immediately began a snowball fight that lasted all the way to the park. Caroline was happy to see that Jo's scarf was the perfect color to contrast with her parka, and Peter's scarf seemed the perfect color for him as well. When his cousins snowballed him and tried to draw him into the fight, he declared he was protected from snowballs by his magic scarf, and stayed with Jo and Caroline to help ensure the little ones got to the park safely. Caroline secretly rejoiced.

Sleds left over from Jo and Peter's childhoods were put to good use by the younger cousins, while older cousins continued to throw snowballs, tackling each other and stuffing snow down fronts and backs. Peter, Jo, and Caroline helped the youngest to have a good time, picking them up when their sleds tipped over on the hill and hauling them back up the hill from the bottom. Occasionally, they took advantage of an available sled and went down the hill themselves. It wasn't a steep grade, but everyone had a great time. Due to their high-spirited antics, it was the older cousins who began to beg to go home to get warm and dry. They hadn't come prepared for rollicking in the snow and some were packing snowballs with bare hands. Josh and the other young ones were reluctant to leave the sledding, but were ultimately persuaded to return to the house for peppermint ice cream and Christmas cookies.

Caroline gladly accepted a cup of hot chocolate once everyone had shed their cold, wet belongings in the Berkhardts' entryway. The adults had already returned to their tables with fresh coffee, or perhaps had never left, and the children eagerly filled any empty chair they could find at first. Eventually, they were sorted back to their places and ice cream and cookies were handed around. Caroline had loved every minute of the sledding fun, and quite naturally followed Jo and Peter's inclination to take their dessert with them to the basement rec room when the swarm of older kids thundered down the stairs.

Peter immediately challenged one and all to a Ping-Pong tournament, systematically beating one after another of his cousins. Caroline kept an entertained ear tuned to the boisterous competition. She happened to love table tennis, but doubted that she could beat Peter. Still, she'd like to try.

37

"Who's next?" inquired Peter, having beaten all of his cousins. "Step right up. Come on, Jo. Caroline?"

"No thanks," laughed Jo. "I learned a long time ago I'll never beat you."

"Caroline! Your turn!" Peter declared, handing her a paddle and ball, which she accepted with trepidation. "You may serve first!"

"Okay." Caroline gathered her courage. "Ready?" Caroline started with a serve to the far edge of the table that took Peter by surprise. There was no way he could have returned the serve. It was her best shot and she had opened with it. She laughed at his exaggeratedly stunned look in spite of the knowledge that he would soon find she couldn't maintain the lead.

"Go, Caroline!" shouted Jon.

"Three out of five games!" grinned Peter, wondering if he was going to lose the game.

"Three out of five!" Caroline agreed with a laugh.

The serves and volleys continued rapidly, with Caroline just keeping the lead. She was doing her best not to let him win. With the score ten to ten, she managed to use her best serve again and catch him unable to return, winning the first game. The cousins went wild.

"Peter! She beat you!"

"Peter let a girl beat him!"

"Gentlemen, I protest! Peter exclaimed. "I did not let her

beat me. She won fair and square! Get ready for my comeback!"

Caroline focused with intensity on keeping up with him at his flat out best in game two. It wasn't easy, and she fell behind, losing game two by two points. Peter won game three quickly and easily. She refocused and gave him her best game, winning game four more by luck than skill. Game five was a brief battle, but Peter steadily drew ahead, winning with long-practiced finesse and strength. The cousins cheerfully declared Caroline the winner when she really wasn't, razzing Peter about being beaten by a girl. They made good use of the situation to inflict pretend humiliation on their favorite cousin. Peter and Caroline cheerfully ignored their teasing and relinquished the paddles to the younger ones now clamoring to play one another.

"That was great! Thanks for the games!" Peter exclaimed. "Where did you learn to play?"

"One of the families I lived with had a table," she explained modestly, not revealing that she'd practiced relentlessly in those days with anyone who would play, and still went out of her way to play anytime she could. She'd found a dismantled Ping-Pong table leaning against the wall in her grandparents' basement, so she'd set it up and had practiced her serves whenever the endless studying made her restless, but she'd had no idea the Berkhardts had a table.

"I reserve the right to regain my championship standing,"

Peter warned, continuing his cousins' joke. "Next time I won't be letting you win!"

"Oh, right, Peter!" exclaimed Jo. "She gave you a run for your money!"

"You're right. She did!"

"It was fun! Thanks, Peter. You won fair and square," Caroline acknowledged with a smile, hoping her competitive playing wouldn't discourage him from future opportunities to play.

What was left of the afternoon passed quickly for the exuberant crowd in the basement, with a variety of games and activities to occupy them. Eventually the kids were called back upstairs, resulting in a rush of feet on the basement stairs as they joyfully responded, perhaps hoping for more goodies; but as darkness fell, Jo and Caroline lit the dozens of candles they had scattered throughout the main floor of the house days ago when they had worked so hard together to decorate for Jo's mom, and everyone gathered around the piano to sing Christmas carols. With Jo and Peter's mom at the piano and their dad leading, a full choir of voices joined together to sing the oldest, most beautiful stories of Christ's birth. Caroline had heard Christmas carols before, had sung some of the snappier ones in high school, and had even been to church with some foster families to sing them at Christmas time, but none of that had moved her as this experience moved her. Not only did she feel accepted, but for the first time, she understood the depth of meaning that gave such beauty to the traditional carols: their beauty grew out of the message of God's love, of God's ultimate gift, of Christ's coming and suffering, of his death and resurrection, of the looking ahead to eternal life with him. New faith in her heart illuminated the ancient words with clarity and simplicity, as many of the hymns they sang in addition to the traditional carols added layer on layer of truth. They sang verses she had never heard, of even the most familiar carols:

Then let us all with one accord
Sing praises to our heavenly Lord
That hath made heaven and earth of naught
And with His blood mankind hath bought.

Noel, Noel, Noel, Noel
Born is the King of Israel.

How blessed Caroline felt herself to be as she participated, allowing the melodic music with such rich meaning to fill her emptiness. This was the heritage she now claimed. This was what it meant to be part of the family of God.

CHAPTER THREE

The next morning, Caroline was eager to get out of bed in spite of the previous day's festivities. There had been a full evening of Christmas caroling followed by supper tables loaded with the remains of the turkey and all of the sandwich-making components to be desired. Cookies of all kinds overflowed the serving plates, including Claire Berkhardt's gingerbread men so perfectly decorated that they looked like Christmas ornaments waiting to be hung. Caroline's toffee, thanks to her Grandmother Emily's recipe, had been a highly-prized success and was completely devoured; and by the time Jo drove her home, she was more contented than she ever remembered being. Sleepy from the full day of feasting and celebration, she'd still managed to get a few things done before enjoying a good night's rest. This morning she resolved to begin thinking about a car. Was there any way she could afford one?

After yesterday's feasting, Caroline took the time to prepare only a minimal breakfast of Greek yogurt and fruit.

She intended to ask the Lord what to do. She didn't want Jo to have to keep driving her around, no matter how much she disliked the idea of the expense and trouble of driving, not to mention maintaining, a car. The coldest part of winter was yet to come, and it would be nice to have the flexibility and safety her own car would provide.

"Well, Lord, I have a big need. I know you answer prayer, so please help me figure out if I can afford a car. One that will get me safely and cheaply through school for as long as I need it. Thank you for all the delicious food yesterday, and for Jo and Peter and their family. Please bless this food," she concluded. "In Christ's name, Amen."

She knew little about cars and certainly had no favorites. She'd truly had very little automotive experience, only learning to drive the Axels' dilapidated van out of necessity. They probably wouldn't have let her drive it so often if they could have managed it themselves. It had been sold for a few thousand dollars when Mrs. Axel went to live with her sister after Mr. Axel died, and there had been little opportunity to drive anything else. She had no idea where to start looking, or what kind of car she would like to drive. She supposed a small used sedan like Jo drove would be most practical.

Early that morning, she had briefly browsed online for cars similar to Jo's, but she was appalled at the prices even for used ones. She wasn't at all sure of the optimal age of a car when the price dropped significantly and the car would still be sound without frequent or extensive, costly repairs. No doubt it completely depended on the make and model. Before deciding on a purchase, she would need to be sure that the car would make life easier for her, not more complicated. She needed advice from someone. Maybe Jo's grandfather could help. She hadn't anticipated seeing a car as a genuine need in her life.

Caroline picked up her grandmother's Bible. She read John 9:30-34, her devotional passage for the day, containing the words of the man born blind whom Jesus had healed. The devotional guide pointed out that Jesus could provide both deep spiritual healing and physical healing.

"What is my deepest need right now?" the study asked. "Is Jesus willing and able to meet my deepest need?"

Suddenly, Caroline was confronted with her deepest need: not a car, not physical healing like the man born blind, but healing of her spirit. She knew that God was asking her to let go of her anger and bitterness and resentment toward God, toward her family, toward all of those foster families, and toward all of the people in her life who had labeled her as a foster child, those who had judged her of little consequence, of questionable character, or as someone to be pitied. She knew the only way that could happen was if she could somehow forgive them all. God could take care of a need such as a car, but this was a true need deep within her, a need that had driven her for nearly as long as she could remember, and only God could touch this need. Other questions in the study guide swirled before her tear-washed eyes. Would she ever be done crying? She had rarely cried while enduring years of loneliness and resentment, and now she seemed to cry at the drop of a hat!

"What do I consider an affliction in my life?" the study guide asked. "What would God's healing in that area look like in my life?"

She knew immediately what it would look like and sound like: thankfulness! Her heart cried out to God in fear and inadequacy. Could she turn the resentment of all those years toward all those people, into thankfulness?

"Please help me, God! I forgive them. Help me to be grateful for them instead."

That was all she could say, but it stood for so much more that was happening within her. She had come to realize that growing up in foster homes was God's way of answering her grandmother's prayers for her protection and salvation, but she had never dreamed that she could ever see the sum total of her experiences as a true gift from God, as something for which she could ever be thankful. In an instant, God now revealed all that he had given her through her difficulties: she was an entirely different, stronger, and more well-equipped person from the person she would have been if not faced with all of the hardship she had endured. From that realization, God, in his graciousness, took her one step further. She could even look back with gratitude, not only to God, but to all of those "strangers" who had helped her on her way. She had hardened her heart to them, but now she was grateful in the way she knew many of them had expected her to be, but she had until now been unable to be.

"Thank you, Jesus," was all she could say.

It seemed such a holy moment, as though Jesus stood right there in her grandmother's breakfast room with her.

"Thank you, Jesus, for each one of them. For what each one of them did for me, for what each one taught me, good or bad, for all that I learned from them."

In the space at the bottom of the study guide page, she wrote to Jesus all about it, even though she knew he already knew. He was the one who had made her the strong, independent person she needed to be to come here to find her true heritage and claim it for herself. When she finally set aside her morning devotional, it was as though a song deep within her carried her joyfully through her numerous tasks. She was so grateful to God.

A morning of exciting progress on her sewing project was nearly over when she decided to take a break and check out the garage. She'd only glanced in the side door to make sure everything was secure with the first big snow. It wasn't a place she'd planned to spend any time, but maybe she should try the garage door openers and make sure everything was in working order. Taking the keys from the hook by the back door, she reminded herself that she and Jo intended to work on the "flower room" to make it more like the rest of the house. There was no way Caroline was going to call her back entry the "mud room" when it was stocked with her grandmother's exquisite vases and accumulated flower arranging tools. She still had trouble believing that she was the owner of all this.

The garage door remotes had no batteries, so she was grateful when she found one new battery in a drawer. There was no way to know how long the battery had been sitting in the drawer, but she really only needed to open the main double door. Hopefully this one still had enough power to operate the opener.

It was a crisp, sunny, winter day. Deciding she may as well enjoy the snow, Caroline took the time to pull on the new snow boots she'd found on sale just before Christmas. They were lined with warm fuzzy fleece that felt snug and cozy today. She zipped her parka as she pulled the back door closed behind her. The garage was detached, but only a short walk from the south end of the house. With a push of the button on the remote, she was relieved to see that the double garage door facing the cul-de-sac worked! She walked in, really for the first time, and looked around the two-car area that was large and empty except for a few shelves with automotive bottles and cans stored on them. Remembering the fun they'd had the day before, she wondered if sleds and other leftovers from her mother's childhood might have been saved and stored away somewhere by her grandparents. She walked toward the back corner where the connecting door led into the third bay. If anything remained from her mother's childhood, it might be in there.

The third bay, perpendicular to the rest of the garage, had a one-car garage door exiting on the side opposite the house, and the wall separating the third bay from the main garage made it impossible to see into it. She thought she'd seen legs to covered patio furniture when she'd glanced in last fall. Now she walked through the connecting door and took the time to lift the coverings. She was pleased to find a large set of very expensive tables and chairs as well as lounge chairs and side tables. It was going to be so much fun to put them out in the spring, on the stone patio at the back of the house! She couldn't wait for warmer weather!

She had made a lot of promises to herself about next summer. Down the path at the back of the yard there was the boathouse, needing a coat of paint, with the canoe and the neglected rowboat safely stowed for the winter. She eagerly awaited launching them on the small lake that joined the Lockwood property with hers. And maybe she should start looking at seed catalogs to figure out what she would grow for her first garden! It would give her a head start if she knew what and when to plant. She could so easily imagine the greenhouse filled with densely-planted healthy seedlings, seedlings she could start while still waiting for warm weather, but she doubted she would have time to make use of the greenhouse this year. Maybe she should wait until after the freeze date and plant directly into the raised beds. Next year, or after finishing her degree and gaining some practice with different plants to see what grew well, she could really go all out.

There were some floor-to-ceiling cupboards behind the patio furniture, with space above them filled with sleds and skis of some kind. She would need a ladder to get to them. Boxes were piled high to the left of the patio furniture. It was dark in the third bay, even with the other part of the garage wide open. It looked like there were a couple of bikes hanging on the partition wall. What a find! Maybe she would get them down and see what kind of shape they were in. On second thought, maybe she'd wait until spring. The garage was cold.

Caroline made her way over to the boxes, wondering what they contained. She stared beyond them into the gloom punctuated by a thin crack of daylight underlining the single garage door of the third bay. A tarp covered something long and low, centered in front of the door. It didn't seem big enough to be a car. So low! So small. Certainly not big enough for a car! Her mind reeling, she turned back to the light switches and flipped them all on. Then she picked her way through the patio furniture again, holding her breath. Those were definitely tires, and there was most definitely an exhaust pipe sticking out the back! Lifting an edge of the heavy tarp, she stood looking at a very small car, nose to the side garage door she had never bothered to open. She held up the back of the thick tarp and stood dumbfounded, looking at the chrome bumper and the shiny, deep green paint above it. It looked spotless. There was a logo on the trunk lid. "MG." What was that? She had no idea! "MGB," said a smaller chrome logo above the large MG. She folded the tarp back a little more on the side, to reveal flashy wire wheels and nearly flat tires.

"I guess it's been sitting here a while."

She lifted the dense, cloth tarp and tried to dislodge it further, revealing a rich, tan-colored, leather covering securely fastened across the top of what was obviously an open convertible.

"It didn't have to be a convertible!" she exclaimed, shaking her head in disbelief. How amazing! God had provided a car, and it looked like a very special one. She lifted the tarp a little more, and then circled the car, checking the other tires. "Pretty flat!" The body, however, seemed to be in perfect condition. She wanted to see if it had an engine under the hood, but she was afraid to touch the strange, immaculate car. Was it drivable? Was this really God's answer to her prayer? She had never had a desire to drive a sporty little convertible! Maybe God meant for her to sell it and buy something practical. She would definitely need help figuring this out!

51

Caroline retraced her steps over and between the boxes and stacks of odds and ends she had not yet explored, and walked out to the front of her "empty" garage. Where had this car come from? John and Martha Lockwood might know. Turning toward their house, she stepped through the undisturbed snow covering the extensive lawns of the two homes. Sunlight turned the undulating white carpet into a field of sparkling gems. Perhaps, to God, reflected snow glory was as valuable as the glitter of diamonds. After all, he could make either with little effort on his part. Hadn't he produced a car when she needed it?

When there was no answer to the Lockwoods' doorbell, she called Jo instead. Would Jo's family know anything about it?

"Jo, I've found a car in my garage!"

"A car in your garage! What do you mean?"

"I found a car in my garage!"

"What is it? Where did it come from?"

"I don't know. It's a little convertible. It's beautiful. It's an MG."

"An MG? Peter, what's an MG? Here. Peter wants to talk to you."

"Peter? I found this car in my garage."

"You found an MG in your garage?" he laughed.

"I guess so. I don't understand! I mean, I've looked in the garage, but never in the third bay across the back. It was way at the back, or the front actually, at the door on the south end. And it was covered with a tarp."

"I seem to remember your grandfather driving something sporty. Is it a green roadster?"

"Uh... It's a dark green convertible."

"Two door?"

"I think so. Yes."

"Could we come over and see it?"

"Please! I'm afraid I don't know anything about cars. I need help figuring out if it's drivable, or if I could sell it."

"Hold on a minute."

Caroline waited until Peter came back.

"Could Jo and I come over after lunch?"

"Sure."

"Oh, wait! We'll bring fast food with us if you want."

"Great!"

"What would you like?"

They spent some time deciding which place to stop, and Caroline gave Peter her salad choice. When she'd hung up, she did a search on her phone for MGs, attempting to get a quick education. It was a British car. So, was the steering wheel on the wrong side?

"The convertibles are called roadsters!" She wondered if Peter had known she didn't have a clue what a roadster was. He had been kind enough not to press the subject, and he hadn't even kidded her about not knowing she had a car in

53

her own garage. She felt so foolish! What would Peter think of her?

At least I won't have to cook lunch! It would be nerve-racking to cook for Peter and she wasn't sure she had anything suitable on hand. She was so glad Jo was coming!

When Peter and Jo pulled up in front of the house, they could see the open garage, seemingly empty.

"That's got to be the cleanest garage I've ever seen," observed Peter.

It wasn't until they walked into the garage that the legs of the covered patio furniture became visible where the back wall ended in the corner. They still didn't see a car.

Caroline had seen them pull up in Peter's car and joined them as quickly as she could, pulling on her parka. "Here. I brought the garage door opener for the third bay around on the south side. We'll have to go out and around the side of the garage. I only have one battery for one opener, so I had to switch it over to this one. I hope it works."

"I can see why you assumed the garage was empty!" Peter assured her.

"I had noticed the patio furniture, but I'd never actually been in the third bay," Caroline explained.

"MGs aren't very big," Peter said, excusing her ignorance of the car in her garage. "Especially covered with a tarp in a dark garage."

She pushed the garage door opener as they walked

around the south side of the garage. "Oh, good! This opener works, too!"

"Nice!" exclaimed Peter, as they pushed and pulled the rest of the awkward, dusty tarp from the car. Caroline was relieved to see a bump out, or up, built into the leather covering for the steering wheel. Thankfully, it was on the American side of the car.

"It's a classic! Look at those wire wheels!" Peter was obviously enjoying himself. "I'll bet it has the wood steering wheel! I think my prayer won!" he laughed.

"I think you're right!" laughed Caroline. "But I don't know if I should keep it or sell it." A wood steering wheel? What did he mean?

"You should keep it!" Peter advised.

"What if it doesn't work?" Jo asked.

"Well, let's find out. There's a compressor here. I'll see if I can get some air in the tires. Caroline, if it's okay with you, I'd like to push it into the double garage so I have plenty of room to work on it. Is that okay?"

"Sure!"

"We'd better eat first." Jo recommended. "We're going to have to shovel the driveway."

"Do I have to?"

"What? Eat or shovel the drive?"

"Both!"

Caroline and Jo laughed as they headed toward the house

55

with the food. Peter jogged ahead of them to open the storm door. It didn't take long for them to seat themselves at the kitchen table where Caroline had set places for them.

"Would you pray, Peter?" Caroline asked.

"Thank you, God, for this food. Bless our bodies with it. Thank you for answering my prayer for Caroline to have a cool car to drive, and help me to get it running for her. In Christ's name, Amen."

Jo and Caroline were trying not to laugh.

"Peter!" exclaimed Jo.

"What? God has a sense of humor. Besides, he can answer both our prayers."

"I know! You're right," Jo conceded.

"So tell me about MGs. I'm totally ignorant," Caroline admitted.

"Well, let's see," Peter began. "Yours is an MGB. They were made only for a certain number of years, by a British car manufacturer, to replace the MGA. We'll have to see what year yours is. They stopped making MGBs in 1980."

"So it's old! It might not be the best car to drive. Are MGBs rare and expensive? Maybe I could sell it."

"They aren't exactly rare, and not worth excessive amounts of money. Here, let's see what we can find." He typed "MGB" into his phone's search engine. "Here we go. 'MGBs for sale,'" he said, showing Caroline and Jo some of the cars and prices that came up. "It depends on the mileage, what kind of shape they're in, how much of the original car remains, and how it's been restored. It looks like your grandfather spared no expense. I would say, if it runs, you should drive it rather than sell it. I don't think you would get a lot for it if you sold it, but I'll be able to tell you more after I've looked at it and gotten it up and running."

"Can we help?" Caroline asked.

"Sure! I'm hoping your grandfather left some tools for us. I've brought the toolkit I keep in my car. Grandpa John will probably have anything else we need. If we're lucky, the tires will hold air. They were pretty low. But I'm anxious to see how it runs. I'll have to drain the oil and gas first. And then it probably needs a new battery."

"Keys!" exclaimed Caroline. "I don't know where the keys are!"

"Keys would help!" Peter laughed.

"You check the study! I'll run upstairs."

Jo was left behind to clean up the remains of their lunches. Peter seemed quite at home, she realized, as he went straight to the study and began rummaging in Caroline's grandfather's desk and then moved on to other possibilities. She could hear him quickly searching through doors and drawers. As close brother and sister, Jo and Peter had often known what each other thought, but it was the first time she had seen Peter and another girl on the same wavelength, and there had been a lot of girls who'd tried. She had to admit

57

that it felt a little like she was losing Peter, but she had long ago come to grips with Peter growing up and apart from her. Still, this felt different than Peter having his own friends and choosing to do things with the guys, even different than him going away to graduate school. Jo reminded herself that it could have happened years ago. Peter could have found a girlfriend long before now if he had wanted to. Thankfully, Caroline was already her friend. Besides, what if Peter had gone for some shallow, giggly airhead or a high-society-type bombshell instead! Jo had a lot of respect for Caroline and liked her immensely.

I wonder what will happen. I wonder how soon it will happen. Would it be a year, maybe a shorter time, or more than a year, before they were married? Jo scolded herself, coming back to reality. She was getting way ahead of them, so she automatically turned her musings into prayer. "Please do what's best, Lord. Thank you that I get to be part of this. Please work out what's best for them." *Do I have the maturity to be a friend to them both but to stay out of their story and let God work it out?* It would be tempting to help their romance along. Better to let it unfold over time. She could even be wrong about them, but there was no precedent in Peter's life that she knew of. There wasn't really any history of Peter's attachments that she, as a sister, could refer to as good or bad, as passing or permanent. Peter had always said he was waiting for the right one.

Caroline brought down a set of keys on an MG key ring from a drawer in her grandfather's bedside table, and they all hurried back outside.

"Allow me, ladies!" Peter tackled the drive with the only snow shovel in Caroline's empty garage.

"I'll go borrow Grandpa John's snow shovel," Jo volunteered, taking off.

"Great idea!"

"I don't think they're home," Caroline called after Jo.

"Okay. I can get in anyway!"

Caroline found a worn-out snow shovel in the third bay, and began to help. It wasn't long before Jo came back with two good shovels, and progress began to come more quickly. Working in the sunshine, the temperature seemed slightly warmer than Christmas day had been, but with the brisk air they enjoyed being warmed by the exercise. Eventually, they had the broad two-car drive cleared and a narrower width down the south side of the garage also cleared.

"I'm glad your grandfather had a cement drive poured down the side! And it's a good thing you girls got that workout," Peter teased as they set aside the snow shovels, "because I'll have to sit in the car and steer while you push."

"Think again, bro!" exclaimed Jo.

"Just kidding. I'll steer and push at the same time. If you can push from the back, this should be pretty easy. See how kind God was to give you an MGB, Caroline? How many people can push their cars these days? It's so small, if it breaks down, you just push it to the nearest garage!"

Jo punched Peter in the arm, on behalf of Caroline, as they headed back to the MG.

"Let's get this tonneau off," Peter said, unsnapping the leather cover on the driver's side. "Look at the wood steering wheel. Perfect! And the wood gear shift knob!" he exclaimed.

Caroline was relieved and pleasantly surprised. The wood steering wheel was large, but it didn't look as strange as she had feared it would. It was made of a beautifully-grained wood, and she actually believed she might like it.

It took some time online for Peter to find the correct air pressure for the small fourteen-inch tires, and then it took more time to fill them.

"Well, it looks like they're all holding air," Peter affirmed. "At least for now. Time to see what you girls are made of. Did you eat your Wheaties this morning? Salads for lunch aren't going to do the job!"

With a great deal of laughter, they managed to roll the MG out of the garage, where it overshot the narrow, shoveled pathway and headed into the snowy lawn.

"I thought you were going to steer!" Jo couldn't help but tease.

"Let's roll it back a little so I can straighten it out."

Once the car hit the slope of the front drive, Peter had to

act quickly to prevent it from rolling all the way down to the street.

"The brakes work!" He was happy to report the obvious. This was followed by a hilarious attempt by the three of them to back the car up the slope and into the open garage. When this nearly impossible task was finally completed, the car was far from centered, and parked at an angle, but it was in!

"Whose great idea was *that*?" Peter asked, as they stood breathlessly around it.

A honk from the street interrupted their recovery as Jo and Peter's grandparents pulled up in front of Caroline's drive.

"Is that Jack's MGB?" asked John Lockwood. He and Martha climbed out and came to see.

"We saw you all, and Peter's car out front. What's going on?" asked Martha.

"I found this car in the third bay back there," explained Caroline.

"I thought he sold that years ago!" exclaimed John. "He asked me if I wanted to buy it, but I didn't think we needed three cars."

"Well, it's fortunate you didn't buy it. This is God's answer to our prayers for Caroline. She needed a car!" explained Peter.

"So Peter prayed for her to have a cool car to drive!" explained Jo.

61

"Yes, and my dear sister prayed for her to have a good reliable car to drive," Peter said with a grin.

"Well, I guess it could be both," observed John Lockwood. "MGBs aren't known for their reliability, but it was Jack's pride and joy. He put a lot of money into it. It used to purr like a kitten, but I guess it's been sitting here for a while."

"We borrowed your snow shovels, Grandpa," Jo interjected.

"That's good. But I think you might need more than snow shovels to start it up. You're welcome to use anything you need out of our garage, Peter."

"I'd like to drain and replace the oil and gas first. I'll have to check around for a new battery. Once that's done, we can try to start it up."

"Well, like I said, Jack spared no expense, so I don't think you'll have any real problems. Come on over, and we'll find something for you to put the old oil and gas in."

Grandpa John placed a friendly hand on Peter's shoulder. A kindly smile warmed his comfortable face, and Caroline was filled with appreciation for the way he so obviously loved his grandson. How grateful she was for these people! And what a nut Peter was today!

CHAPTER FOUR

Grandpa John drove Martha over to their garage while the rest of them walked next door where Jo and Caroline were soon weighed down with a variety of odds and ends that Peter and his grandfather thought necessary to the MGB's health. Back in Caroline's garage, they lifted the hood. Peter whistled.

"It's immaculate!"

"He had the engine rebuilt," reminisced Grandpa John. "Put in all new wiring. He went for the best paint job he could get. In fact, he spent so much on the car he couldn't get his money out of it when he started advertising. He used to say he wished he'd gone with red paint and a black interior because he thought that looked snappier. Then he decided what he really wanted was an Austin-Healey."

"What's an Austin-Healey?" Caroline asked.

"Oh, it's a little fancier British sports car. Costs a whole lot more than an MGB. Really classy!"

"Well, I'm glad he didn't sell it or paint it red. I like the

63

deep green," observed Caroline.

"It's called British Racing Green. This was an extra deep green that he chose."

"It's perfect!" exclaimed Peter. "Never was a red sports car fan, myself."

"Me either," agreed Caroline.

"Here's the VIN number," Grandpa John pointed out to Peter.

"Let's see what year it is," Peter said, entering the number as Grandpa John read it to him. A minute later, he enlightened them. "It's a 1973."

"Is that good?" asked Caroline, hopefully.

"I'll have to do a little research later and let you know."

It didn't take long for Peter to start the oil draining. Grandpa John insisted on starting the gas siphoning, knowing he had more experience at the rarely-used skill than Peter. Caroline and Jo were busy trying to get a good look at the interior. They unsnapped the remainder of the leather cover, removing it completely while trying to stay out of Peter and Grandpa John's way.

"It's beautiful!" exclaimed Caroline, touching the rich tan leather seats and the brand-new-looking carpet that matched the color of the seats and cover. It might even be fun to drive, but she would definitely need to practice when no one was around. She wasn't sure she wanted to admit to Peter that she had never driven a stick shift before.

"*That* is a really retro dashboard," she laughed rather dubiously.

"Yes, but not complicated. It's a simple car, unless your grandfather altered it substantially," commented Peter.

"He kept it as near collector perfect as he could," insisted Grandpa John. "It's as close to original as possible, but he upgraded the leather and carpet. That was one of the things the purists didn't like about what he did. He said they wanted the original leather seat covers with contrasting edges. Piping I guess they call it.

"I don't think I'd like a contrasting color. I really like this," Caroline said, running her hand appreciatively across the luxurious leather.

"I think he called it a biscuit color," Grandpa John informed her.

"Dual carburetors! Where's the battery?" Peter asked, with his head under the hood again.

"Ahh... if I remember right, they're over here behind the seats."

"They? More than one battery?"

"Seems like that's how they came. I think maybe Jack altered it."

Peter did a quick search online. "Wow! They came with two six-volt batteries until 1974!"

Peter and his grandfather managed to pull back the thick, upgraded carpet that covered the floor behind the seats. A lid was screwed down behind each seat.

"According to these online posts, we have to be careful not to strip out these screws," Peter warned.

Under the first lid, was a box containing a few tools and polishing cloths.

"Yup. I believe he converted it over to one twelve-volt battery," said John. "We should find it under this other lid."

Sure enough, a single twelve-volt battery occupied the space under the lid on the other side of the car.

"It looks like a lot of people convert them to one battery," said Peter, scrolling through some online postings. "That sure makes it easier on us. It means we won't need special batteries," he explained to Jo and Caroline. "We can easily buy a good battery locally without a lot of trouble or expense."

"What will a battery cost?" asked Caroline.

"No worries. I think I'd better make a trip for gas, and oil, and a new battery. My treat, since I prayed such an irresponsible prayer! Want to come, Grandpa?"

"Oh, I can't let you do that," Caroline protested, wondering how much all of this was going to amount to. She had a feeling they were just getting started.

"I insist!" Peter stated with a smile. "I've found the battery nearby, so it shouldn't take long. See you later!" He and Grandpa John were already headed to Peter's car.

"Better replace the transmission oil, too," Grandpa said.

Peter was making notes on his phone. "Oil filter, air filter, spark plugs… "

Troubled, Caroline followed their conversation until they were in Peter's car, driving away.

"Let's ask Grandma if we could make some hot chocolate," Jo said, stomping her cold feet.

"Do you want to call her and see if she'd like to come over? I have a hot chocolate recipe I'd like to try and lots of cookies to get rid of!"

"Okay!"

"Grandma Martha says she'll be right over," reported Jo as the girls headed toward Caroline's back door.

"We could decorate this room with your favorite flower. What *is* your favorite flower?" asked Jo as she pulled off her boots.

"I have lots of favorites, but white calla lilies are a possibility."

"White callas are so elegant!"

"Um-hum. Maybe too elegant for a room like this. I just don't know how to make this room special."

"Wall paper? Some kind of textured finish on the walls, maybe. Or photos of callas. Framed prints, or maybe watercolors?"

"I just can't picture it yet. I want it to be unique and beautiful, but not too fancy."

"We'll think about it. We could start collecting online

pictures of white callas and any similar rooms you like."

"That's a good idea. Eventually it will come together. I haven't had time, and probably won't until next summer. Maybe spring break. I guess I could start an idea board, though."

They talked about various shades of green or blue, or maybe yellow, that might work for the walls, as they prepared the hot chocolate. Grandma Martha knocked on the back door, and they helped her remove her bulky coat and scarf.

"Hot chocolate is just what we need! Thank you, Caroline," she said, accepting a warm cup from Caroline.

"Do you want to text Peter and tell him we'll have hot chocolate for them when they get back?" Caroline asked Jo.

A minute later, Jo reported that Peter and Grandpa John had already stopped for coffee, so there would be no need for hot chocolate. Thanks anyway, but they were anxious to get to work when they got back, to see if they could get the MG started. It would probably take several hours.

"Jo, I'll have to pay Peter back. Can you help me get the receipts?"

"We'll see. I think he deserves to cover the expenses!" Jo laughed.

They explained to Grandma Martha that Peter felt obligated to pay for the things he needed to get the car running because of his prayer for a cool car. Martha hid her surprise, knowing Peter's own budget was tight enough.

"It gives Peter and his grandfather a project to work on together. That's a gift from God right there!" she said, trying to reassure Caroline.

"That's right!" exclaimed Jo. "Let's see." She picked up her phone and read a text message. "They're at the parts store. Peter says you'll need to find the papers on the car so you can register it in your name and get new plates. He says the title isn't in the car, so you'll need to see if your grandfather has a file on it. Hopefully, the title will be there. You also might want to call and find out what proof they'll need that the car is yours."

Caroline went to her grandfather's study and, after quickly locating the MGB file, checked to make sure that the car title was there. If she had ever noticed the file, it had not had meaning for her before today, but now that she knew what an MGB was, and that it was hers, she perused the file with interest. There was information about its original condition and innumerable records for all of the work her grandfather had done. After she made the phone call to the motor vehicle department and collected her grandparents' death certificates and other required information, Jo and her grandmother decided to drive her over to get the title transferred and get new plates for the car. It was a long process, but in the end, Caroline was registered as the legal owner of the MGB. She tried not to reveal her shock at the fees she'd had to pay for the classic car to be legal and on the road year round. Instead of revealing her need, she sent up a silent prayer.

"Lord, you provided the car, so please provide all that's needed. I just spent all of my budget for January and more. I'm going to need money, Lord."

Martha decided to go home and rest, so Jo stayed with Caroline, waiting for the new parts to be brought back. When Grandpa John pulled up next door, Peter texted Jo that it would be a while before they had anything to show them, so they might as well stay warm.

The afternoon passed quickly for Caroline. She'd never had a close friend who made it so easy to talk and share the things that mattered to her. She showed her grandmother's third-floor retreat to Jo, who had never been there before. Caroline pointed out her grandmother's journals that had been so influential in Caroline's salvation. She showed Jo the photo portraits of her mother and some of the rest of the family pictures. They spent a long time at the broad windows that overlooked the lake and forest, a novel perspective that fascinated Jo and set her to identifying everything she could see.

Jo discovered Caroline's stash of gazebo catalogs and they began avidly comparing the advantages of different models and companies. Caroline pointed out the perfect location at the edge of the yard behind the house and explained that she had always wanted a gazebo. She had promised herself a large, elaborate one when she got her first job. Jo was intrigued with the designs, and they took turns investigating the features of their favorites.

Later, they played some of her grandparents' music and ended up in the basement working on Caroline's sewing project, which turned out to be providential as Jo was able to pin the skirt hem for her.

When Peter texted that they were about to start the car, they ran for their coats and eagerly appeared in the garage. Caroline had grabbed the paperwork from the motor vehicle department to show Peter.

"Very cool!" Peter commented with a grin.

"You're going to need insurance. Would you like our agent to give you a call?" Grandpa John asked. "He's a good guy and I doubt if you'd beat the cost significantly anywhere else."

"I guess that would be a good idea," Caroline agreed. She tried not to show her anxiety, wondering if it would cost a small fortune to insure a vintage classic car like this. If she was going to drive it, she was going to need insurance.

"We're just about ready to try to start it up. Could be a few more minutes."

Peter and his grandfather had already been working on the car for hours! How could she ever repay them? She was beginning to wonder if it was worth all that they were putting into it. Would it really start? Half an hour later, they all stood around while Peter climbed in to give it a try.

"Okay, Lord! Thank you for answering Peter's prayer. Please answer mine, so Caroline has a car to drive!" Jo prayed out loud.

"Ready?" Peter teased before turning the key.

"Ready!" Caroline smiled, holding her breath.

"Here we go!"

On the first attempt, the car turned over… but didn't start. On the second, it caught and roared to life.

"It works!" cheered Jo, jumping up and down. "Thank you, Jesus!"

Caroline's grin was wide. In fact, Peter remembered it later that night after he'd gone home and stored it in his memory as a reward for his labors. Seeing Caroline smile like that was worth any amount of effort.

"Sounds a bit rough. What do you think, Grandpa?" he asked.

Peter eventually sent Caroline and Jo back inside to stay warm, explaining that it would take some time to adjust the carburetors and the timing. He would let them know when it was ready for a test drive. The temperature seemed to be dropping, and they were both very willing to retreat to Caroline's house to talk and look at her sewing projects.

"I think that's good," Grandpa John decided some time later. "Seems to be running fine. You might want to give it a try around the cul-de-sac before letting the girls know."

"Maybe I'd better put the top on and turn on the heater."

He retrieved the convertible top from the garage shelf where he had seen it earlier and he and his grandfather fastened it on, beginning at the back and figuring out how to evenly spread it up and over the car to fasten above the windshield. Peter rolled up the windows, turned on the heater, and circled the cul-de-sac a few times, getting used to driving it while it warmed up. Jo and Caroline pulled on their coats and came to stand beside Grandpa John until Peter pulled up.

"Shall we take it for a spin?" he asked.

"Okay!" Caroline agreed.

"Is there room for me in the back?" asked Jo.

"Only if you're a contortionist," Peter joked. "I think you can squeeze in if you fold up your legs."

They laughed as Jo attempted to make herself comfortable in a back seat that was never intended for passengers.

"You'd better drive," Peter said to Caroline. "It's your car!"

"I'd rather watch you first. I've never driven a stick shift."

"You can do it! I'll help you."

"I'd rather you drove so I can watch first, if you don't mind."

"Okay. Hop in!"

They started out slowly, Peter explaining everything he did. He seemed very comfortable with the car, though he also seemed to fill every bit of space in the driver's seat. Caroline tried to adjust her thinking to accommodate its peculiarities as they circled the cul-de-sac.

"Why is the steering wheel so big?" she asked.

"There's no power steering! You're going to have to become a muscle woman," Peter joked. He braked and explained the gears on the gear shift knob, then demonstrated smooth shifting with the clutch again. "Your turn! Let's switch places."

Caroline would have preferred not to demonstrate her first attempts in front of Peter, but she had to drive this car sooner or later, so she swallowed her pride, telling herself that he seemed to be a patient teacher. Perhaps he wouldn't mock and tease too much!

"Let me out first, please!" Jo requested. "I'm scrunched!" More laughter accompanied her efforts to extricate herself from the cramped back seat.

Caroline went around to the driver's side, waving to Grandpa John who stood watching from the driveway.

"You can do it, Caroline!" yelled Jo encouragingly.

Caroline climbed in, surprised at how comfortable she felt in the driver's seat. It was cozy, not claustrophobic. And it felt just her size. She put it in first, trying to ease up on the clutch and press the accelerator at the same time. The MGB gave a jump and promptly stalled.

"Happens to everybody," Peter consoled as Caroline laid her head on the steering wheel in embarrassment.

"Really?"

"Truly. Just remember, this is God's answer to our prayers, so it will be all right."

"Really?"

"Really. Start it up. It's good practice."

She managed to start it and get it into first gear, then second. Peter insisted she practice several times before putting it into third. The oversized cul-de-sac was a great place to begin, but before long it would begin to limit her progress.

"Do you want me to park it? I'd like to back it into the garage so I can work on it some more," Peter explained.

Caroline pulled over and jumped out, relieved that her first driving lesson was finished. Thanks to Peter, she was no longer worried about being able to drive it. She just needed more practice.

Peter and Jo left soon after because their mother didn't think she could delay dinner any longer. Caroline asked them to apologize to her for taking up the entire day. She was profuse with her thanks to Peter and his grandfather.

"I never thought I'd be working on Jack's MG," chuckled Grandpa John. "Had a great time!"

"Thanks for your help, Grandpa. I learned a lot!" Peter said. "That's a pretty fun car!"

When Caroline returned to her sewing that evening, she replayed the day over and over in her mind. Peter couldn't have been too upset with her driving. He seemed happy to suggest that he return in a couple of days to help her with another lesson and to make sure the car started and ran smoothly. She felt so ignorant about cars. She'd had very little experience driving! It was probably the car itself that was the attraction for Peter, she reasoned reluctantly. He seemed to really enjoy working on it. That's what guys did!

The next day she spoke to the insurance agent that John Lockwood had recommended. She could get other quotes, but she guessed his estimate had to be in the ballpark. She simply didn't have the money, so she told him she would call him back when the car was drivable. Peter and Jo weren't coming today due to previous commitments, but they would be back the next day. She'd better see what she could do about covering some of these expenses. She had discovered a set of files in her grandfather's study that seemed to be labeled with many of the treasures in Grandmother's display cases and other places in the house, so she was curious to see what information it contained about the two masks from Venice. It helped that Jo's grandmother and her friend Millie Larson had been so adamant that these particular souvenirs her grandfather had brought home from a business trip had not been well liked by her grandmother.

When Caroline found the correct file, it contained a general description of the masks and a receipt that caused her to exclaim in surprise. She never would have guessed what her grandfather had paid for them! He had evidently purchased them from a high-end shop in Venice. She wondered if there was any way a jewelry store in the area might be able to sell them. Maybe they would purchase them from her, or sell them on consignment to the right customer. If they weren't interested, she would have to try to sell them herself online. Either way, she was sure to have to take less than the purchase price unless the gold and jewels had appreciated considerably. It was possible that they had, but the masks were only gold-plated so rises in the price of gold couldn't affect their value that much. There was no way to find out if anyone would buy them and what they were worth if she didn't step out of her comfort zone and ask. She'd have to risk being cheated. She prayed for guidance, looked for comparables online, and finally went to John and Martha with her dilemma.

Martha was soon on the phone with a friend whose daughter worked in a jewelry store, and soon after that, on the phone again leaving a message for the daughter to call her. It wasn't long before Martha was explaining to the daughter that these items a friend of hers wished to sell were not something to sell to the buyers of gold to be melted down. They were unique works of art, worth a considerable amount. The friend's daughter left the phone for a brief time and then returned to say they could bring the items to show her boss. He would make no promises, but he was willing to look at them.

"Let's go, John!" Martha exclaimed when she finished explaining to John and Caroline. "Let's drive right over there and see what this Mr. Sitchel thinks!"

"I guess we could, if Caroline wants to."

"I don't want to interrupt your plans for the day. You worked so hard on the MG yesterday!" Caroline protested.

"No, now!" exclaimed John. "That was just plain fun! Besides, I did take a break or two when Peter wasn't looking."

"And we didn't have any plans today. Let's go!" Martha insisted. "Your grandmother always wondered how in the world she would sell those things if she decided she really needed to. If it will help you, let's get it done!"

An hour later, the three of them were seated in the office of Mr. Sitchel. Caroline pulled the elaborate masks gently from the bags in which she had carried them and laid them on his desk. She handed him the description and the receipt and explained that she wished to sell them.

He took his time examining them with a jeweler's glass, rubbed his jaw, and looked at them some more.

"I do have a client who may be interested. That's the only

possibility I can think of. If I could send him some pictures, we could see if he's interested. I'll get back to you. I would expect a fifty percent commission."

Caroline tried to hide her shock at the percentage he would take. She knew of no other way to sell them, so she agreed to allow Mr. Sitchel to photograph them, a process that took some time because he wanted to get them in good light with a black velvet background. He arranged them a couple of different ways, took several shots of them, and explained that he would send them to his client.

John Lockwood paused to shake Mr. Sitchel's hand on the way out, "You let us know if your client is interested. We'll be offering it to other sellers as well, so you may want to rethink that commission. Thank you for your time."

Back in the Lockwoods' car, Martha and Caroline giggled over John's nerve.

"Well, I have an idea," he explained. "Remember when I purchased your new rings? I think we should try Mr. Kharine over at that jewelry store."

"Oh, they did do a very nice job, didn't they," Martha agreed, looking down at her wedding rings. "I didn't know you knew anyone there, though."

"I looked at several diamonds to choose the best ones. The manager, Mr. Kharine, was very helpful."

"You did pick such nice ones, John," Martha said, showing Caroline the results. "Isn't it nice, Caroline? For our forty-fifth anniversary! Thank you, Honey."

John smiled at Martha, and Caroline found herself wondering at their relationship. They seemed happier than many married people. They were kind people. You could see kindness in their faces. She was sure they had been faithful to each other all of these years, and their children also had successful marriages and families. They were the most unselfish people she'd ever met. Was that part of the answer to a successful marriage? It was definitely what Caroline wanted out of life. She wanted to practice the selflessness now that would help her find the right person and help her maintain that relationship for forty-five years and beyond. She wanted to be the right person, herself, to fit into that kind of marriage.

"Please, Lord," she prayed silently, "help me to be that kind of person. Someday, help me be ready for that kind of marriage."

They were able to meet with Mr. Kharine after a brief wait, and he ushered them into his office to talk. When Caroline showed him the masks, he also said that he knew a client who might be interested. His commission would be twenty percent. He took some pictures and promised to call Caroline when he had anything to report.

"Thank you, Mr. Lockwood," Caroline began, as they walked out of the store.

"What did you call me?" John Lockwood asked with a

funny expression on his face.

"I think Grandma Martha and Grandpa John would be much more appropriate," said Martha.

"Well, I should think so!" exclaimed John.

Caroline laughed, embarrassed. Somehow, she mostly avoided addressing them by their names, unsure whether to use first or last names. She had called them John and Martha, but she would never have presumed to use Jo and Peter's familiar form of address, in spite of the Lockwoods' insistence that they were her "adopted" grandparents.

"Are you sure? I don't want to offend your real family."

"Oh, no fear of that. I think they're perfectly willing to share us," laughed Martha, taking Caroline's arm. "We're used to answering to Grandma and Grandpa."

"I... I'll have to try to get used to calling you that," Caroline stammered.

"You'll just have to get used to it," John said, "if you want us to respond. We don't respond well to Mr. and Mrs. Lockwood. Not when it's Jack and Emily's granddaughter we're talking to."

Caroline smiled. "Thank you. You've been so kind to me. I didn't know how to go about selling these silly masks. I appreciate your help."

"Well, we'll see," said Grandpa John. "They aren't sold yet."

Before they left Caroline in front of her house, they made

her practice calling them by their new names. When Caroline left them, it was with a smile on her face. Had they realized that she had never called anyone by the name of Grandmother or Grandfather, face to face? It was something quite foreign to her, but they had taken away the strangeness of it by their friendly insistence. What amazing people they were!

"Thank you, God, for the Lockwoods. Grandma Martha and Grandpa John," she said out loud. It seemed a little less strange than the first time she had said it, but it still seemed presumptuous.

CHAPTER FIVE

Jo called early the next morning. "Hey, Caroline, do you have ice skates? Peter thinks it's been cold enough lately. The lake might be frozen enough to skate."

"Really? It did get awfully cold last night. There were a couple of skates in my mother's room. I mean, my room. I guess they were my mom's. I'll have to try them on. I'm not a very good skater."

"That's okay. Call me back and let me know if they fit. We have some extras and Grandma and Grandpa do, so let me know."

"Okay. I've never skated on a lake. I've only been to an ice rink a couple of times."

"You'll love it! We'll have to shovel the snow off and test the strength of the ice. Make sure your skates have room for warm socks. It's pretty cold out. We'll build a bonfire. Grandma and Grandpa have a firepit down by the lake."

Caroline found some heavy socks and tried them with the skates in her mother's room. Still a little big. Maybe another sock layer would help. She decided one of the sets of skates worked fairly well with two socks. What could she wear to stay warm?

It wasn't enough that she needed Peter's help to learn how to drive her own car. Now she had to reveal to Peter another skill in which she was totally lacking. Ice skating was one thing she'd not had much opportunity to pursue. Wouldn't it be impossible to skate on a bumpy lake? She could barely stand up on a groomed rink! She hated to admit it, but she wasn't thrilled about being out in the cold, either.

Caroline layered as much clothing as she could under her warmest coat, stuck the second pair of socks in her pocket, and hung her skates over her shoulder. Peter and Jo were next door getting the shovels and the wood for the bonfire. When Caroline arrived with her shovel, Peter had already made a trip down to the shore to break the trail through the snow and to carry as much as he could. Caroline carefully piled his arms full of more chopped wood from the Lockwoods' stack, and they set off with Jo and Caroline carrying the special shovels Grandma and Grandpa Lockwood supplied. Caroline had never been down the path to their side of the lake, so she enjoyed the tramp through the woods and looked around with interest when they arrived at the firepit. A rise of wooded land to the right blocked any view of her part of the lake. She wasn't sure whether she should feel regret or be relieved that the two properties had been arranged for seclusion. It was disappointing not to see her house, but she did value privacy.

Peter scooped as much snow out of the bowl-shaped indentation as he could before beginning to lay the foundation for the fire. He had obviously done this before.

"Come on, Caroline," Jo said. "Let's see if we can shovel the snow off."

Jo walked down the slope to the shore and slowly followed the tracks Peter had made earlier, out onto the undisturbed snow that covered the lake.

"How is it?" Peter asked.

"So far so good!"

"It seemed pretty solid. Go parallel to the shore until I can check farther out."

Jo stopped a few yards from the edge of the lake and began to shovel.

"Here, Caroline, you take over here and I'll go farther down and work back toward you," she called.

"Okay."

When Caroline had lifted the snow from a small space and scraped it as clean as she could, she was surprised at the smoothness of the ice. She had expected much rougher bumps and lumps. There were some, of course, but it looked more feasible than she had feared.

"How deep is the water here?" she asked Jo.

"It's a rapid slope down from the shore. I think it ranges between five and eight feet. Grandpa John wanted everybody to be able to boat and swim and skate but without having to worry too much about it getting too deep. It's not a gradual sandy beach like yours. I think your grandfather must have brought in sand and built the beach, but Grandpa John had our cove dug out so there was uniform depth. The water's pretty sheltered here, so it stays calm. We used to have a raft anchored out a ways for swimming."

That explained the smooth surface, Caroline realized. She tried to imagine Peter and Jo as children, or even their mother as a child growing up here. They must have had a lot of fun together as a family with swimming, boating, and fishing in the summer and skating in the winter. She was beginning to get a rhythm to her shoveling but, in spite of the relatively smooth ice, her rhythm was often broken due to irregularities. It was not easy, but she and Jo slowly worked their way toward one another, met in the middle and began working their way back toward their beginning places. Peter had the fire roaring by then and came to join them, working on the next row. He worked as fast as the two of them combined.

Caroline hoped she was doing it right! She checked with Jo when they met up on the next row, and was reassured by her that Peter would go over it again in the opposite direction and clean it up a little more.

"One more row?" Jo asked Peter.

"One more!" he answered.

"Let's get our skates on!" said Jo after they had cleared another row. She and Caroline stood by the fire and watched as Peter went slowly back and forth the other direction, scraping as much snow from the ice as he could and chipping off a few protrusions.

"There's a rough spot here!" he yelled.

"Okay! We'll go around it!" Jo shouted back as Peter continued his work.

Jo and Caroline added more wood to the fire, enjoying its warmth.

"Time to skate!" Peter called with the biggest grin Caroline had ever seen on his face, as he carried his shovel up the slope toward them.

"The tricky part is getting your skates on without getting snow on your socks!" Jo explained to Caroline.

They sat on the benches that Peter had cleared, and managed to get their skates on without too much trouble. Caroline tightened hers as much as she could. Were Jo's skates different from hers, or was she just used to doing this? Jo seemed to be ready much faster with considerable less effort.

"Do you mind if I pull those laces up tight for you?" Peter asked Caroline. "It will make it easier for you to skate."

"Sure. Thanks!"

Peter removed his gloves and knelt in the snow. Caroline stared at his broad shoulders, then at the top of his wavy, dark hair. He was wearing his new scarf, but no hat. She watched his strong, deft hands pull the laces tight, one by one. Her ankles felt firmly encased when he was finished. He was careful to ask her if he'd pulled them up too tightly. She tried not to think about reaching out to touch his hair and avoided meeting his fun-filled eyes that seemed so close. She tried to focus on preparing not to make an idiot of herself. Her skates felt comfortable now, and it made her feel more confident about trying to skate.

"We'll see," she told herself. Actually standing up and then trying to *stay* upright remained to be seen.

Jo and Caroline sidestepped down the slope and held onto each other as they stepped gingerly through the snow toward the cleared ice. Peter finished putting on his skates and joined them about the time they stepped out on the homemade rink.

"Easy," he admonished. "Try just walking at first. Just like you did to get here."

It was good advice, and Caroline was relieved to find that she could walk on the ice without falling. Jo and Peter shoved off, trying a few short excursions, and then came back to her.

"It's not too bad," Peter observed.

"Not bad at all!" Jo agreed.

"I don't know!" Caroline looked apprehensive. She was out of her element.

"Try a little skating with us on each side," suggested Peter.

He and Jo each took one of her arms, and she was able to glide a short distance. It was fun!

"This is how I learned to skate," said Jo. "With Mom and Dad holding me up, or Grandma and Grandpa. They took turns until I could do it on my own."

"I seem to remember doing my fair share of holding you up," teased Peter.

"So you did!" Jo admitted comfortably.

Jo and Peter alternated between spotting Caroline on each side and skating off to test out the ice on their own. This must be what it was like to grow up with brothers and sisters and extended family, Jo realized. She was grateful for Peter and Jo's help. It was humbling, but at this point it was the only way she was going to learn how to skate and enjoy it the way they seemed to. She intended to learn to skate well enough to keep up with Peter. There must be plenty of girls who could skate, and she didn't want Peter to have to skate with them just to have a good time.

In what seemed only a short time later, they heard Grandpa John calling from a spot beside the fire.

"Come and get it! Grandma sent lunch for you!"

"Yay! Thanks, Grandpa!" shouted Jo.

They headed for the shore and carefully sidestepped up the slope. Grandpa John had brought more firewood, sandwiches, hot chocolate, and s'more makings.

"Stay and have lunch with us, Grandpa?" asked Jo.

"No, I'll go back and have lunch with your grandmother. It's too cold out here for her. Only you young ones are crazy enough to do this!" But the grin on his face suggested he was totally on their side.

Caroline had never dreamed it could be so much fun to be outdoors in the winter. They ate the sandwiches and drank hot chocolate standing up, as close to the fire as possible; and when it was time to assemble the s'mores, reluctance to remove their gloves created laughable, clumsy attempts. There were roasting forks for the marshmallows, but no matter how careful they were, the marshmallows often flamed up and blackened before they could blow them out. It didn't matter. The s'mores were delicious.

"Cold?" asked Peter.

"Yes!" Caroline and Jo answered together.

"Are you up for one more turn around the rink before we head back? What do you think, Caroline?"

"Sure!" Caroline answered.

They put out the fire, covering it with snow, and headed down the slope toward the lake. Peter leaned into a racing position and began circling their rink but quickly spun out on a turn, sliding into the uncleared area. They all laughed as he stood up, brushing snow from his jeans and coat. Caroline was cold, and skating a few circles around the ice didn't really bring the warmth back to her feet. She was glad when they decided to call it quits. It felt good to remove her skates, but her cold boots didn't do much to help either. After checking the fire carefully, they picked up the shovels and everything else they hadn't used and headed back up the path.

"Did you like it?" Jo asked Caroline.

"It was great!"

"We should do this again tomorrow while the cold lasts. We've done all the work," Peter suggested.

"I don't know, Peter!" Jo said. "I'm tired! I might be stiff by tomorrow!"

Caroline laughed. "I may not be able to stand up tomorrow, skates or no skates!"

"Okay, we'll see how everybody's doing in the morning."

They put the shovels away, left their boots by the door and swarmed into Grandma Martha's kitchen.

"There's more hot chocolate," suggested Grandma. "Any takers?"

"Yes, please!"

They were soon sitting around the kitchen table drinking hot chocolate and eating Christmas cookies, in spite of the s'mores they'd eaten earlier.

"How about a game of Scrabble?" suggested Grandma Martha.

"I'd like to start up the MG and see how the tires are

doing. I'm going to have to leave in a couple of days, so I'd like to make sure it's running well. Why don't Jo and Caroline stay here and get warmed up. Do you mind if I go over and take it for a drive?" Peter asked Caroline.

"Sure. My keys are in my coat pocket. Here they are. The garage door opener is on the counter just inside the back door."

"Is there a receipt for the tires in your grandfather's file?"

"I don't know. I don't remember seeing one, but I wasn't really looking for one either."

"Do you mind if I look?"

"No, I don't mind. I think I left it on Grandfather's desk."

"Okay. I'll come and get you so you can drive it again if everything is working,"

Caroline sat down to a game of Scrabble. She would rather have gone with Peter. Why was he so worried about the tires? They appeared to be in mint condition with plenty of tread, and she thought they'd been holding air.

Peter walked toward Caroline's house, thinking hard. In two days he would have to return to school in order to finish his doctorate and begin applying for jobs. He'd committed to teaching through the summer while finalizing and defending his dissertation, and wouldn't be free until the fall. He wished frequently now that his school were closer to home. He would have to leave Caroline in God's hands again. He had no idea where he would end up in the fall. He believed he wanted to teach computer science, but he'd also wondered if he should work in industry to gain more business experience first. He had done a considerable amount of teaching while working on his degrees, and believed God had blessed those experiences, but there was no guarantee he would be offered a position anywhere near to home even if he applied. He had gone out of his way to prepare his family for the possibility that he could end up working almost anywhere. In fact, he had even been excited about the prospect of exploring other locations. Now, he didn't know what to think. Caroline had a house, one she was attached to for obvious reasons, and she had degrees to finish. She was not likely to want to relocate. And she was still so young. He didn't know how, but somehow he was going to have to make occasional trips home over the next few months, no matter how busy he was. The MG would provide a good excuse to check in with Caroline. Could he keep the relationship low key until he figured out what was going on with his own life?

He was worried about the tires. They had to be several years old and could be less safe than new ones even if they'd had very little wear. Caroline probably couldn't afford to replace them. Grandpa John had insisted on helping with some of the initial expenses but had also insisted that Peter not disclose his help to Caroline. *Please provide new tires if she needs them, Lord.*

He sat at the desk, looking through the MG file, tracing its history. Fun stuff, here!

"Ah, here we go." He had found a tire receipt tucked inside a folded piece of paper. Just as he suspected, they were ten years old. Not really safe even with the small amount of wear. After looking through the rest of the file, he searched online for tires and then headed out to the garage.

The MG was running well and the tires were still holding air, so the rims were evidently in good shape. He drove it out of the cul-de-sac and around the block, deciding to adjust the brakes before texting Caroline to come out for a drive.

When she got his text, Caroline left Jo and her grandmother playing Scrabble and managed to start the car on her own. She and Peter circled the cul-de-sac a few times with jerky gear shifts.

"You're getting the hang of it," Peter encouraged. "I think the car is safe to drive, but I'd rather you stayed off the highway and the interstate. I think you'll find yourself feeling pretty small compared to the big trucks on the road. I did find a tire receipt. I know they look okay, but they're pretty old and might not be safe at high speeds."

"Oh!" exclaimed Caroline. "I thought they were okay since they were holding air. How old are they?"

"Ten years. The good news is the wheels are in good shape. There's no air leaking around the rims. But tires tend to deteriorate after that many years. Sorry to be the bearer of bad news, but better safe than sorry. Here are some of the options I've found online. I think this place is dependable. Here's the range of prices."

"Is that per tire, or for four?" asked Caroline, apprehensively.

"Per tire. Fourteen-inch. But see this range of prices? Some of these in the lower middle range would be fine. You won't have to spend an awful lot, but I know you might not be able to replace them right away. I wouldn't drive on the highways without replacing the tires, but even then, I'd worry about the big trucks, like I said. Do you think you'll need to drive on the interstate?"

"No, I suppose not. Not really, unless something comes up that's unexpected. It wouldn't help me get to church or to school, or places I usually go."

"Good. Do you want to replace the tires right away or wait a bit?"

"I might need to wait a bit."

"If you had a blowout at high speed, it could be dangerous, but if you're just driving between here and church and school, it should be okay until you can replace them."

"What do I do if I have a flat, or a blowout?" Caroline asked, taken by surprise at the entire conversation.

"Your grandfather made sure there's a good spare in the trunk. I've checked it and it seems okay. So, you're really going to need *five* new tires. And I think it would be wise to get roadside assistance with your insurance. It will cost you a little, but then, no matter where you are, you can get help. Can you do that?"

"I suppose. I haven't arranged for the insurance yet, so I won't be driving it yet anyway."

"Promise you'll get roadside assistance?"

"Oh, I suppose." Caroline's penny-pinching independence suffered as she reluctantly agreed.

"It would be best if you replaced the tires before you started driving at all. And will you let me know if you have any trouble with the car?"

"When do you go back to school?"

"Day after tomorrow."

"I don't want to bother you. I don't know what you could do from so far away."

"I'll find a way. Promise to tell me?"

"Okay. I guess."

"Grandpa John will help you, but if you need something, I'll find a way," Peter said.

<hr />

Caroline tried not to miss Peter. He had not come by or called before leaving town. She focused on mapping out her senior project, trying to spend as much time as possible moving ahead with it. She read ahead to have a good start on her upcoming classes. She went shopping with Jo, finished a couple of sewing projects, played her piano, and practiced her Ping-Pong serve. She and Jo even tried another skating session, but it wasn't the same without Peter. She did some research on the life of tires, and decided it was probably for the best that she couldn't drive it yet. She couldn't pay the insurance. Then, one day, she got a call from Mr. Sitchel. His client's offer was low, really low, and with his commission she would not have enough for tires and insurance. She told him she would get back to him and called Mr. Kharine.

"They did look at the pictures," he informed her. "Let me see if I can get them to come in and look at the actual masks."

He called the next day, explaining that they wanted to see the masks. Could she bring them in?

The Lockwoods drove her to his store half an hour before the customers were due to arrive. Mr. Kharine handed Caroline a claim ticket for the masks and they went off to have lunch, praying for a miracle. A short time later, Mr. Kharine called with an offer. It was considerably higher than Mr. Sitchel's, and with the smaller commission, she would have more than enough to cover insurance and tires. In fact, it would put her budget back on track and perhaps allow her to repay some of what Peter had spent. She agreed to the price and told herself not to feel guilty about selling the masks. Her grandmother had not liked them and neither did she!

Later that day, she ordered the tires, paid the insurance, and rejoiced that God had provided a car for her to drive. Now, if she could just drive it without stalling it every time she shifted gears!

Caroline put the MG into first and eased off the clutch, gently pushing on the gas. It died. She had to get it to the tire store today, and after that there would be no excuse not to drive!

"Okay. More gas. I just need to give it more gas!"

She tried it again, this time successfully, and shifted into second before stopping at the stop sign. There would be plenty of stop signs along the way and plenty of practice shifting.

When she was safely at home again, the car sporting brand new tires, she texted Peter to let him know.

"Great!" he replied.

"I'm insured and still have enough to repay you for some of the things you paid for to get the MG running."

"No thanks! Enjoyed working on it. Have a great semester!"

And that was that. She didn't know that Peter called his Grandpa John to make sure the car was in shape now that she was actually going to be driving. She didn't know he had been praying about the tires, concerned about her safety and on the verge of buying them himself. She didn't know that his limited communication was due to the fact that he didn't trust himself not to make promises he couldn't keep.

CHAPTER SIX

Caroline wanted to show Dr. Calton the progress she'd made on her senior project and get his feedback on the direction she was going. When she entered his office for the appointment she had arranged the first week back at school, he greeted her with a smile and listened with interest as she presented her work.

"This is impressive, Caroline. You've taken it much further than I expected."

"Do you have any recommendations?"

"Yes. You should polish what you have here for your senior project. You should pursue this process, this part of it, and set aside the rest for your master's degree."

"Oh! I was afraid I would have to come up with something entirely different for my thesis."

"No, I don't think so. You've laid out enough to carry you right through to the end. In fact, this part of your senior project is the perfect preparation for the rest."

"Wow! That's great! Thank you!"

"Don't thank me! You've done the work."

"But it's so encouraging. I can focus on this area and develop the rest of the code later, then? That helps a lot!"

"Yes, I'd say you're on the right track. How did last semester work out for you? How are things going?"

"Great, I think!"

"Glad to hear it."

"I need to thank you for your calendar," Caroline said with a grin.

"My calendar? Oh yes, I remember you had some connection to the verse that month."

"Yes. I had read it that morning in my devotions. It was all so new to me. I didn't understand what a Christian was, but I do now. I gave my life to Jesus during Christmas break."

Dr. Calton's eyes lit up. "You did?"

"Yes. I think you know the Lockwoods from church."

"Oh, yes!"

"Their granddaughter, Jo, is a friend. She and I are working through the John devotional I was doing."

"Sounds good," Dr. Calton said, nodding his head. "But she's over at Wield Christian U, isn't she?"

"Yeah."

"There are a couple of good Christian organizations active on our campus. You might check them out. You know Jeff Balin? He heads up a Christian leadership team. They coordinate efforts between the organizations and have some good activities in the dorms, too. Weekly Bible studies, I think."

"I'm not sure I have the time. I live off campus. Next to the Lockwoods, actually."

"Oh, that's right. But you might enjoy some of the activities, and they're always a good place to bring friends who aren't involved in a church."

Later, Caroline thought about Dr. Calton's words as she walked across campus to her parking place. She had valued her independence, her privacy, her anonymity. She'd wanted to focus on her degree and not get caught up in campus events. She didn't really know anyone from campus very well, but maybe she should be friendlier. Maybe she could impact someone else's life, someone who needed what she had found.

There was a skinny, scruffy-looking guy slouched against the MG, practically sitting on it, smoking a cigarette.

"Hi, Princess. Are you the owner of this magnificent car?" he asked as she approached. He didn't bother to stand up.

"Excuse me," she said, stepping around him to open the door. She threw her pack into the passenger seat, slid in, and locked the door. She started the car and waved as she backed out, forcing him to stand up.

"Hey, Princess, can you give me a lift?"

"Sorry," she mouthed as she drove off.

What a line! She didn't like being rude, but she knew that was the only way to protect herself. There was no way God would want her to put herself at this guy's disposal. Let one of the Christian guys witness to him. She knew what he would think if she tried to be even slightly decent to him. Maybe it would be a good idea for her to get to know the Christians on campus so she could point them in his direction. She sent a swift prayer up for his salvation and was brought back to wondering if there was someone *she* should reach out to. Was there anyone in her classes who needed to hear the gospel? No doubt! But could she do that? It gave her food for thought, so she began to pray about it.

The Gospel of John was now her daily lifeline to God. At the end of each week, she and Jo discussed what they had learned that week. The study guide seemed to be filled with encouragement to share the gospel with others, now that Caroline was aware of the need. When she called Jo to discuss that week's passages from John, they began to talk about ways to share the good news about Jesus.

"Part of it is being open to the Holy Spirit's leading. I sometimes pray that God would direct me to the person who is searching for him, and to show me how to help that person find Jesus," Jo explained. "It's hard to do that on a Christian campus. I spend more of my time here just praying for God to show me people's needs and ways I can help any of my

Christian brothers and sisters. I have to be more deliberate about getting off campus and taking the time to be involved in other people's lives. That's one of the reasons I help out at the mission whenever I can."

"If I invited someone to a Christian event at the university, would you be able to come, too?"

"Sure! I'd try!"

"Okay. Thanks, Jo."

"You bet. I'm happy to help any way I can."

"I know. Thanks!"

Caroline's time quickly became consumed with classwork. Most of her classes were just what she wanted, and she thrived on the required work. Every day brought her closer to graduation, closer to her graduate degree, closer to achieving her goals. She reached out to a few of her classmates, knowing now that time invested in people was not wasted time. She knew that was how Jesus would want her to think, but it took extra effort. She was perfectly happy going to class and spending as much time as possible working on course content, her senior project, and projects around the house. When she didn't need to be on campus, she was happiest at home.

She loved the solitude, the peace, the amazing gift of having her own home. It was her personal retreat, her avenue to time with the Lord, a place where she could be her naturally happy self. When she opened the door and stepped inside, she often thought of the first time she had done so. Leaving her unhappy past, she had come with her few personal belongings to search for the inheritance that she had thought would make her happy. She had thought she would find her proper place in her own family, something she had longed for growing up in a variety of foster homes, but it was finding her place in God's family that had brought her the happiness for which she had longed. Now, when she was alone she felt God's presence, and there was nothing lacking.

Snow fell throughout the night, but the sun broke through the next morning while Caroline was eating in her grandmother's breakfast room decorated with white wicker and pastel floral paintings. She loved this room. She loved every room in her house, but this one was perfect for sunny winter days. After breakfast and her time with the Lord in Bible reading and prayer, she pulled on her snow boots and parka. This sparkling Saturday morning was the perfect opportunity for a walk down to the lake: the air was brisk and the sunlight brilliant. She found herself jogging down the pathway to the frozen lake. Should she clear the ice and try skating on her own part of the lake? Why not?

Much later, she put on her ice skates and carefully pulled the laces up, section by section. She had tried skating at a nearby rink but was discouraged by the number of kids whizzing around. Not only were they unpredictable, they seemed to skate so effortlessly! Here, she could practice without anyone darting in front of her or swooping past when she felt so wobbly and unsure. It didn't matter what she looked like when there was no one to see, and if she could skate on the uneven lake, she could skate anywhere. She was actually beginning to enjoy it.

As she walked back up the hill for lunch, her skates over her shoulder, she looked around the woods. Her woods! She didn't want to ever get over the wonder of being the owner of all of this. Barren deciduous branches reached toward the sky, enabling her to see the ruffle of evergreen trees in the background. She remembered the arrogant thought she'd had when she first came, that she would protect and surround her property, like those evergreens. Now, she knew better.

"Lord, please protect and surround me and this property. I can't do it without you. Thank you for all of this. Thank you."

When spring came, she would walk the property boundaries, something she had never done. She looked forward to really exploring the woods that appeared to fill the acres extending beyond the house. From her grandmother's third-story study, the woods looked dense and unending and, though the property was fenced, the woods appeared to blend into neighboring properties without a break. However, she was fairly certain that the scattered line of evergreens extending straight west from her back yard followed the fence outlining the north edge of the property. She could see that the evergreens took an abrupt turn to the left on the other side of the lake, most likely following the fence outlining the western edge of the property.

She hoped that tonight she could eat in her grandmother's study and watch the sunset. If the clouds that were creeping in front of the sun didn't move in too densely, tonight could be a colorful display. She had been too busy studying lately to take time for the sunset, and she missed the beauty she had promised herself when she first discovered the glorious sunset view. She remembered how surprised she'd been to see those third-story windows from the lake path below, how she had hurried back inside to find the door, how she had found the key in an envelope addressed to her, and how she had discovered her grandmother's journals. Perhaps it was time to start writing in that blank journal Grandma Martha and Grandpa John had given her for Christmas.

That evening after dinner, eaten in the company of a glorious sunset, she sat at her grandmother's desk, looking at the blank first page of the elegant journal she had been given. Where should she start? How much did she have to reveal? And who would be reading this? Her grandmother's journals had been locked away, but Caroline didn't intend to write anything that she would mind becoming public knowledge.

She put the date at the top of the page and began with the earliest memories she had of her mother and father, her grandmother and grandfather. She would not dwell on their faults and sins. Instead, she wrote of the loving times she remembered.

> *These are the memories that brought me here to this house. I know now that God is the source of all that is good. He brought me here to discover him when I needed him the most.*

It was late when she closed the journal and put it aside. Her eyes were wet with tears, yet her heart was filled with contentment. She hoped she would never forget those early childhood memories, but when she was elderly and forgetful, perhaps there would come a time when she would take this out and read it and be glad that she had recorded what little she had to remember at this point.

The next evening, she began writing about the foster families who had taken her in. She had no memory of the first few families. She remembered feeling lost without her mother, accompanied by memories of clinging to her father. And then had come the feeling of being utterly destroyed inside when informed of her father's death. It was his death that had cemented the black hole created by the devastation of finding herself alone in the world. Being surrounded by total strangers was something that had taken her a long time to overcome, but over time she had developed coping strategies. She was able to hide her emotions and pretend everything was fine. It made life simpler because then the people around her acted normally and just let her be. Nothing they did or said helped. Nothing consoled her grief. It was better to be left alone and treated as though her life were normal. How could she ever write about the pointless attempts at comfort by women who weren't her mother?

"I can't do this, God. You'll have to help me," she prayed, putting the journal aside. She just couldn't do it. Not yet. Maybe never.

Caroline hurried out the doorway of her last class for the day, anxious to get home. It was her busiest day of the week and she and Jo had brought some friends to one of the Christian events on campus the night before. She had some catching up to do that evening and was hoping for a good sunset. One of the Christian students she knew stopped her in the hallway.

"Hey, Caroline, I want to introduce you to Jeff Balin,"

"Great to meet you, Caroline," said a nice-looking guy. "I saw you last night but didn't get a chance to meet everyone."

"Hi, Jeff. I hear you had a lot to do with last night's event. Thanks for putting it on. It's great to have things happening to invite people to who need the Lord."

"Sure. So you're a believer?"

"Yes! A new one, but all in!"

Jeff walked beside her, continuing the conversation. "Oh? How long? How did you become a Christian?"

"Just before Christmas. My friend Jo led me to the Lord. She was there last night! She's a senior at Wield Christian."

"That's great! How did you meet her?"

"Her grandparents live next door to me." There were depths here she couldn't possibly explain. "I've been trying to get to know more people on campus so I can invite them to your events."

"Cool. Hey, some of us are meeting at Tony's Italian for lunch Friday. We'll probably work on planning the next event for spring. Want to join us?"

"I don't know. What time?"

"Twelve noon. Just come if you can. Hope you will!"

"Okay, I'll see."

When they parted, Caroline reverted to her normal tendency to keep her life simple and focused. She wasn't likely to show up at Tony's on Friday. But when she spent time with the Lord the next morning, she remembered to pray about it. She didn't want to miss out on what God wanted for her, and when she mentioned it to Jo, her reaction was surprisingly positive.

"I think you should go. It's good for you to connect with

the strong Christians on your campus. Besides, you have a lot to offer."

"What do you mean?"

"I'll bet you have some good ideas about meaningful things they could do to reach out to students who need Jesus."

"Yeah, I guess I do, but I'm so new at this. Why should they listen to me?"

"That's exactly the perspective this particular group wants and needs. Just ask the Lord about it and see what happens."

"Really?"

"Yes."

"Okay, but I don't think that's really me."

When Friday noon rolled around, Caroline had just finished a class and realized she could either get in her car and go home or walk the two blocks to Tony's.

"I guess I need lunch anyway," she decided, a little annoyed that she was even considering this. Maybe going once would help settle it. She didn't have to start hanging out with them. She might not be invited back, either.

"Hey, Caroline. Glad you made it!" Jeff greeted her as she approached the table surrounded by four guys and four girls, a mixture of people she knew and didn't know. She was relieved that the few she did know were students she respected, based on her limited time on campus.

Over pizza and salad they all discussed the pizza and movie night they were planning for sometime after spring break. They seemed to have it pretty well planned. Caroline found herself impressed with their organization and selfless commitment: it was evident that they each contributed a lot of time to make these events happen.

Jeff summed it up, reviewing each person's responsibilities and then changed the subject. "The other thing on the agenda today is trying to find a location for our day retreat this winter. Our venue fell through. Anybody know a place where this group could meet for free? Some place where we could meet to plan and pray and have a good time together?"

"Oh, yeah. When was that scheduled?" someone asked.

"A week from Saturday."

"So disappointing," someone else observed.

"Yeah, I was looking forward to that!"

"I did find a room available at the church, but we'd be confined to that one room. They have a major men's event that day," Jeff explained.

"Doesn't sound like much fun."

"Wish we had a home we could use. A roaring fireplace. A place to spread out and relax."

"Yeah, wouldn't that be wonderful?"

"Too bad none of us are local."

Caroline sat quietly, waiting to see if anyone had a

113

solution. She would wait to see if this was of the Lord. She replayed her recent conversation with Jo about the ethics of owning such a large home. Jo had encouraged her to give the house to God to use as he knew best, to hold its ownership lightly in her hands since it was a gift from God and belonged to him anyway, to be willing to part with it if and when God ever asked that of her, and to try to be willing to give it up but to ask God to use it for his glory for as long as she was there. Jo had been thinking of her brother, Peter, but had not revealed her thoughts to Caroline because she told herself that *anyone* Caroline ended up marrying might ask her to move. Besides, wouldn't it be amazing if Caroline and Peter got married and lived next door to Grandma and Grandpa Lockwood?

Caroline waited for the group to come up with a location for their retreat, silently asking God to make her willing if this was the answer to her prayers that God would bless her home and use it to further his kingdom.

"I hate to cancel it," Jeff observed. "Last year it was such a spiritual boost."

"Remember the answers to prayer?" one of the girls prompted.

"Yeah. Tori's friend, Meg. And the brother and sister from Canada."

"What do you usually do at your retreat?" asked Caroline.

"Oh, we start about 10 in the morning with a Bible study

and prayer time, then break for lunch and some fun, and spend a couple more hours planning for the rest of the year and praying. Praying for specific students we know who need the Lord," Jeff informed her.

No one seemed to have any ideas about a place. Every suggestion seemed to be met with complications.

"Would you like to come to my house?" Caroline found herself asking.

"Wow! Really? Oh, yeah, you said you lived off campus. Do you live at home?" one of the girls asked.

"Yes, I do."

"Do you want to check with your parents? We might drive them crazy if they stick around," Jeff suggested.

"My parents died when I was a little girl. I inherited the house from my grandparents. You're welcome to have your retreat there next Saturday if you want."

"Really?"

"Sure. If the cold holds, we could skate on the lake and roast hot dogs and make s'mores for lunch," Caroline added, remembering that the Lockwoods had done the same for at least two generations of Christian groups. "We can have a roaring fire in the fireplace. I have plenty of wood," she added, thinking how little of the stack behind the garage she had used, her preference being the ease and cleanliness of the gas fireplace in the library. "I have a Ping-Pong table in the basement."

115

"No way!" someone said.

They looked at her in astonishment. She wasn't quite sure why they seemed so surprised.

"Sounds great!" Jeff said. "Mia, do you have the food lined up?"

"I waited because we weren't sure where it would be. I'll bring donuts for the morning."

"If you want coffee," Caroline informed them, "someone else will have to bring it and be in charge of making it. I don't drink coffee, but I have a coffee maker."

"I'll do that," Jeff volunteered.

"Oh, and it would help if two or three guys could come early to shovel the lake for skating," Caroline added.

"I'll do that, too," Jeff said as two other guys also volunteered.

"I'll bring hot dogs, buns, and all the fixings," one of the girls offered generously.

"I have ketchup, mustard, and relish," said Caroline.

"Okay. I'll bring onions and cheese. And some chili,"

"I'll get a veggie tray for snacking," said another girl.

"I'm really good at buying paper plates," joked one of the guys.

"Throw in some disposable silverware and paper cups and you're on," Jeff recommended.

"I'm all over those s'mores. Got 'em covered!" said another of the guys.

Everything was soon provided for, and Caroline headed home for the weekend to do homework and plan the coming week so that the house would be ready for the event. Jo offered to come the following Friday afternoon to help with the house, and Caroline began to look forward to spending time with the group. She didn't feel the need to tell anyone that their retreat was the day of her birthday.

"Wow! Nice house!" Ian commented as he and Jeff came in.

Caroline showed them where to leave the coffee and other things they'd brought and took them out to the garage for shovels as soon as Drew pulled into the drive. The Lockwoods had gladly offered the use of their shovels, roasting forks, and skates. Behind the garage, Caroline loaded everyone up with as much wood as they could carry. The weather had stayed unusually cold, with low temperatures even for January, and the snow crunched and squeaked under their feet as they walked down the path to the lake.

"What's in the boathouse?" asked Drew.

"Just an old rowboat and a canoe."

"Cool! I'll bet that's really fun in the summer."

"Yeah," Caroline answered noncommittally, not wanting to explain that she had never spent a summer using them on the lake. Changing her mind with the thought that she had nothing to lose, she explained, "I just came last fall, so I haven't tried them out yet. I've been too busy with school and trying to take care of the place. I think the boathouse needs a coat of paint and I'm not sure how seaworthy the boats are."

"Invite us back for our summer planning session and we can fix that, eh, Jeff?" Drew replied.

"Sure. We could have a paint party and have it done in no time at all," Jeff acknowledged.

"Really? That would be great. But… that might not sound like fun to everyone."

"Well, we could check out the boats and do some boating, too."

"That would be great!" Caroline admitted, thinking that they would quickly forget their offer of help. "The firepit's on the other side of the boathouse. See the circle of rocks?"

They stacked the wood they had carried while Caroline walked off the perimeter of the best ice and the three were soon hard at work.

"I'll head back up to the house in case anyone else comes," she yelled so they could hear over their exertions.

"Sounds good!"

She picked up another armload of wood on her way into the house and started the fire in the magnificent family room fireplace. It was nice to have a reason to use the fireplace. By the time it was burning enthusiastically, Josh, Mia, Meg, and Gabbie had all arrived in Lyndsey's car. She showed them where to put everything and listened to their appreciative exclamations. As the girls eventually settled in the family room, Josh decided to run down to the lake to join the other guys.

"Just stop behind the garage and grab an armful of wood," Caroline directed. "If you follow our tracks down the hill, that will lead you right to them."

Once the skating area was cleared and everything was ready, they all gathered in the family room with coffee, tea, or hot chocolate and the breakfast burritos Caroline had gotten up extra early to prepare. Her egg and sausage burritos were enthusiastically welcomed and voraciously devoured. Mia's donuts made the perfect follow up.

Caroline appreciated the morning Bible study that proved to be especially meaningful under Jeff's leadership. The prayer time grew directly out of the study, guiding them to pray more effectively. Jeff seemed to know what he was doing!

By lunchtime, they were all happy to leave their serious work behind and enjoy the sunshine and brisk, invigorating air. Some were experienced skaters and some were totally inexperienced, so Caroline enjoyed giving the beginners empathetic help and was gratified to see that she had progressed since that first day of skating with Jo and Peter.

The guys built a roaring fire, with the result that they all skated as long as they could to allow it to die down enough for roasting hot dogs.

"Man, this tastes good!" Josh said, finishing off his second hot dog dripping with mustard and relish. "Think I need one more."

"So, who thinks we should come back in May and paint Caroline's boathouse?" asked Drew.

"For sure!"

"Sounds like fun!"

"Do you want us back for our final meeting of the year?" asked Jeff.

"That would be great!" Caroline responded.

"Done deal. We'll try to come up with some paint. What color would you like?"

"Pretty much what it is now. A grey-beige with white trim?"

"It does look classy with the rock foundation. I'll see what I can do."

"Time for s'mores!" Mia said, tossing bags of marshmallows into waiting hands.

Clean up was a busy time with everyone helping to put out the fire and carry all of their lunch and skating gear back to the house for a planning session. As they discussed events scheduled for the remainder of the school year, Caroline was able to offer her ideas and could see the thoughtful expressions on faces as she explained her reasoning. The rest of the schedule went quickly, with another prayer time that impressed her: they all really cared about school friends who didn't know Jesus and prayers were very specific for individuals who were experiencing difficulties as a result of their unbelief and life choices. The team wanted them to know the love of God and to find rest from the unfulfilling search for substitutes for a relationship with Jesus. Caroline enjoyed being part of a group that had dedicated itself to providing that opportunity to their classmates. She was really excited about some of the activities they had planned. When they left, she thanked the Lord for giving her the privilege of hosting them and set out cheerfully to restore the house to its usual immaculate order.

The next day at the Lockwoods', Jo and her grandmother began discussing Jo's birthday wish list.

"When is your birthday, Caroline?" asked Jo.

"Yesterday," Caroline admitted reluctantly, knowing they would chide her for not telling anyone.

"Yesterday! Why didn't you tell me! So you're twenty now, right? Did the leadership team know yesterday? Did you celebrate?"

"No. I didn't tell them. We had a great time, and I didn't want to complicate their meeting."

"Complicate their meeting!"

"Well, we're about to complicate our lunch!" exclaimed

Grandma Lockwood. "Nobody turns twenty without some kind of celebration!"

Jo hung up a birthday banner, part of the traditional birthday celebrations at the Lockwoods', and Grandma Martha had a two-tiered cake baking in the oven before they sat down to lunch. She even managed to find the correct number of candles and, after a prolonged lunch and one of Grandma Martha's favorite games of Scrabble, the cake was cool enough to frost. When they lit the candles and sang "Happy Birthday" Caroline managed not to cry, but just barely.

CHAPTER SEVEN

By spring break, Caroline had given up on hearing from Peter. One weekend in February he'd shown up at her door, looked the car over, driven it around a bit, and left. He never called. He never sent a text message and only briefly answered hers. No emails. No messages through Jo. She tried not to mind.

She was grateful that the MGB had worked perfectly through the winter months. Being low and small with rear-wheel drive, it wasn't the best car to drive in the snow, but she had managed. When the snow was really deep, she rode the bus to the university.

The unusually cold winter finally relented, leaving a cold that lacked the bitter intensity to which everyone had become accustomed, and spring break was a welcome relief from studying. She didn't mind that most students seemed to be headed to Florida. There were so many things she wanted to do, and there was only one week.

Caroline loved the church service on Palm Sunday, a

week before Easter. The children's choir sang, "Hosanna! Hosanna! Hosanna in the highest!" It was as though the whole universe knew that Jesus was the Son of God. The Son of God was riding into Jerusalem on a donkey, claiming his rightful kingship, and the very rocks would have cried out if the children had not! Jesus chose the entrance any Jewish king would make, but also the entrance that their Messiah, in particular, would make. Yet he rode in meekly, knowing that he would be betrayed and crucified, humbling himself for our sakes to accomplish God's greater purpose of salvation for all the world!

The pastor explained, "Jesus came in submission to the Father's will, on a donkey, to his people, not on the warhorse of a conquering king. But someday, he will return and it will be as King of Kings and Lord of Lords, when the time is right."

Caroline had lunch, usually referred to as "dinner" on special Sundays, at the Lockwoods' after the morning church service and went home with leftovers that Martha had insisted she take. Jo had been at her own church and at her parents' home for Palm Sunday, but texted an invitation for Caroline to come for Easter dinner, along with the Lockwoods, the next week.

The week off from school was crammed with as much progress as she could make on her senior project. Each evening she reluctantly let go of the day, eager to start the next, but dreading the end of her precious week! She began to hunger, both literally and figuratively, for spring. Though it was still too early in the year to plant her gardens, she poured over seed catalogs and searched online sites before placing careful orders. She couldn't wait to sample her first spring produce.

On Friday evening, Caroline drove to a Good Friday service at church. Certain that she had never attended a Good Friday service before, she wondered if it would be sad or depressing. Instead, she found it to be the most holy experience of her life. Music that was soft and pensive was filled with the power of God and drew all thoughts to the Friday so long ago when Jesus was crucified. As the pastor spoke of Christ's sacrifice, the holiness and the love of God filled Caroline with awe. The service ended with communion, the lighting of candles, one last song, and an uncharacteristic silence that everyone was asked to maintain as they left the sanctuary. Christ's peace filled Caroline as she drove home, reflecting the entire way on how glad she was that she had gone to the service. She had never experienced anything like it in her life and thanked God with all her heart for his generosity in giving his Son and for his mercy in revealing him to her. She remembered how she had doubted God's existence, doubted his love, doubted that he'd had anything to do with planning her life to bring good out of it. How different she felt now that she knew him! She knew

God had answered her grandmother's prayers, especially the prayers on her behalf. No longer doubting God's goodness and power filled her with the sense of security she'd never had growing up without her family. She was part of God's family now and would be forever grateful.

She maintained a focus on Jesus through the weekend by playing a recording of Dubois' *Seven Last Words of Christ*, which she'd heard for the first time at the Good Friday service. The *Second Word* had caught her attention musically and emotionally. As the pastor had asked his congregation, were we not all required to see ourselves in the position of the thief who acknowledged Christ's innocence, Christ's ability to save, and to express humble, heart-felt contrition for our sins? It seemed she couldn't get enough of the tenor and baritone harmony that served as such an eloquent vehicle for the Lord's words to the repentant thief on the cross at his side: *Hodie mecum eris in paradiso. Verily, thou shalt be in paradise today with me.*

On Easter morning she delivered full Easter baskets to the children in the neighboring family around the corner. The surprise on their faces, so quickly replaced by glee, made her laugh.

"Awesome!" exclaimed Andrew, tearing open the wrapping.

"Awesome!" exclaimed his sister Kyla, in such blatant imitation of her brother that Caroline caught a glimpse of what it would be like to have a big brother. She wondered if Jo had imitated Peter when they were kids. They certainly had an easy mutual respect for one another now.

The church service that Easter morning was a joy-filled celebration of the resurrection. Jesus had not remained dead in the tomb! He lived. He lived now! He was her shepherd and savior. He would help her finish the school year. He would provide what she needed. Now that Jesus was interceding for her, she knew she didn't have to do it alone. She had never been afraid of hard work, or of scrimping along with limited funds, but now that she rested in God's loving promise to provide, the daily anxiety and resentment she used to live with had evaporated. She rode to church and then Easter lunch with John and Martha, contented to give this day to honoring the Lord. The Berkhardts had kindly included her in their plans, and she looked forward to Easter dinner.

And there was Peter's car! Knowing that his spring break had been earlier, she was surprised that he had made the drive home for Easter.

"How's the MG?" was his first question.

"Great!"

"Any trouble with it starting?"

"No. It's been great!"

"Any trouble with the steering?"

"Nope. I'm getting used to muscling it around the

corners. And parking's easy because it's so small. Thankfully, I don't have to parallel park."

"New tires doing okay?"

"Yup. No problems."

"Except for the creeps the car attracts," Jo contributed.

"Creeps?"

"Oh, just one. He likes the car and I have to be rude to him every time I find him leaning against it when I come out of class." She didn't mention the annoying habit he had of calling her "Princess" and how distasteful she found his whole appearance and demeanor.

"Is he bothering you?" Peter asked with a frown.

"No. He seems harmless. Just annoying."

Peter didn't look satisfied or happy, but let it drop. Caroline was relieved, hoping he had quickly forgotten it. It was embarrassing. But Peter silently worried through lunch, knowing he was powerless to intervene. He couldn't be there with her! He'd been forced to work through his own spring break which had occurred earlier than Caroline's. With the defense of his dissertation approaching and Caroline busy with her own coursework, he had been somewhat contented at the time, but now he wished he'd come home and shown up on her campus. If only he had known! He had wondered about the wisdom of applying for a teaching position at her university, but there was no other way to be there for her. Could he focus on his job if he saw Caroline every day?

Seeing Caroline every day… the job application was almost complete. He should be able to submit it tomorrow.

"Hey, Caroline, I think I need some help this week while I'm off. I wish our breaks had coincided." Jo had already told Caroline that she was struggling with one of her classes. "Math and I have never been good friends. I shouldn't have put this course off until my senior year!"

"Oh, I'll be glad to help! We can take a look at it after lunch. Then you can let me know if you want to come over sometime, too. Maybe we could meet at the coffee shop before my Tuesday morning class. Or call me if you think we can do it over the phone." She couldn't help but continue. "I guess I feel like math is kind of a window into God's mind. I love it! I've always loved it, but now I know why. It's like we can observe God's creativity by understanding the world in such an abstract, specific way. Everything in the universe can be described mathematically, and mathematicians are always trying to figure out how we can describe what we think is true, using mathematical equations! I don't think there's any end to math. I mean there's always more to discover, more to learn. If God's mind is infinite, and that's reflected in creation, like no snowflake being the same, no person being the same, then math is part of that. I mean, I guess maybe creation is finite at some point, so maybe math is too, but from our perspective there's so much yet to discover we'll never run out of things to learn."

"I never thought of it that way," Jo said.

"And look at physics! It seems like we never fully understand how God did it or how the world really works. But mathematical models get us as close as we can probably get. I think it's entirely cool that God designed a world based on math, a world that can be described using math."

Peter was staring at her with a strange expression on his face. She wasn't sure what that expression meant.

"Sorry!" she exclaimed. "I didn't mean to get carried away."

"You can get carried away any time you like," Peter replied with a smile. "Let's all take a look at Jo's course after lunch."

Jo and Peter's father, Bret, asked Grandpa John to give thanks for their meal. Caroline loved the sound of his voice, the low, full timber rejoicing in this day. He thanked God for this most sacred of all days, remembering the day when the Savior was raised from the dead after his crucifixion, raised on the first day of the week, raised as a "first fruit" or first fulfillment of God's intention to raise to life all who believe in his Son, raised as proof that Jesus is indeed God's Son.

Lunch was wonderful and a much smaller crowd than Christmas! With only Peter's parents and grandparents present, conversation flowed easily as Jo, Peter, and Caroline exchanged updates on their school lives; and with Peter's parents and grandparents wondering what his next steps would be, Caroline listened to their questions and Peter's replies with great interest. What would happen once Peter had defended his dissertation this summer? It was disappointing for Caroline to learn that he was already committed to teaching through the summer term where he was, and Peter thought it best to reveal as little as possible about the possibility of teaching at any of the local colleges, especially at Caroline's university in the fall, or at any point in the future.

He knew that, even with Dr. Calton as a willing reference, there was no guarantee, or even probability, that he could secure a position there for the next year. He had to teach somewhere, and it could easily turn out to be elsewhere, no matter what his wishes. If his parents and grandparents knew he was applying in his hometown, it would only lead to speculation and potential disappointment. They might even begin to speculate about his relationship to Caroline and he wasn't ready for that. It was best to keep it under his hat for now. So he proceeded as planned, unaware that his mother, grandmother, and sister were already praying for what was best for Peter and Caroline. Peter's father Bret was becoming increasingly impressed with Jo's friend, Caroline; and Grandpa John was blatantly asking God to please work it out so that Peter and Caroline could figure out that they were meant for each other, all in God's time of course, and if it was really God's best for them.

When John and Martha decided to go home soon after lunch, Peter and Jo offered to drive Caroline home later, after the intended marathon math help session.

"I have a car so you shouldn't have to do that anymore! Sorry, I should have driven today!" Caroline exclaimed.

"That's okay," Jo said. "I don't mind driving you home."

"I'd like to take a look at the MG anyway," Peter added. "Might need a bit of a tune up by now. Okay if I do that when we take you home?"

"Sure."

"I thought you were driving back tonight," worried Jo.

"I am. It won't take long to make sure the MG's running properly."

"It seems to be running fine," Caroline felt it necessary to say, still hoping that he would come and see.

"I won't be here again for several weeks, so I'd like to check it while I have the chance."

"We'd better get started then! You'll be late getting back!" warned Jo.

But when the math help session was over, time had flown and it was decided that Peter could best begin his long drive back to school more directly from Caroline's house rather than driving Jo home again. Jo waved them off with a grin. They would hardly miss her and she had things to do.

"So tell me about your senior project. How's it going?" Peter asked.

"Great! Dr. C says I'm doing okay, and I can continue it for my master's thesis. The only thing that worries me is dragging it out that long. I'm sure other people are working on similar or totally different solutions that could make it obsolete by the time I finish my master's," she explained, going on to briefly outline her intended direction.

"You may want to file for a patent on your idea."

"Wow! I never thought of that."

"It wouldn't hurt. Software development sometimes takes quantum leaps in unpredictable directions. You could go ahead now and develop it as quickly as you like. The patent would only add to your thesis and look really good on your resume."

"I suppose so. I'll have to think about it."

"Dr. Calton could probably give you some help with deciding if that's really feasible. Patents are tricky. Let me know if you need help with anything. I'm in the process of filing for my first one."

"Thanks! I'll see what Dr. C. thinks."

"So the MG's worked well for you?"

"Yeah, it's been great! Thanks for getting it going for me. I'd really like to pay you back for what you spent."

"No way! I'm just happy my prayer for a cool car didn't land you in trouble!"

Caroline laughed. "No, it's been great!"

Peter checked the oil before starting up Caroline's car.

"It seems to be running smoothly. We could head over to the coffee shop. I'd like to drive it and make sure everything sounds right. I might need some coffee for the drive."

"Sure! I could use some hot chocolate. Let's go!"

"Mind if I drive?"

"No. That's fine!"

An hour later, Peter parked the MG in Caroline's garage and reluctantly said goodbye.

"Remember, let me know if you have any trouble with it. It seems to be running well. I'm glad you replaced the tires. Grandpa said you sold some gaudy gold masks?"

Caroline laughed. "Oh, yes. Fortunately my grandfather gave my grandmother an expensive gift that none of us liked!"

Peter smiled. He loved it when Caroline laughed. "Well, I'm glad it worked out. I'd better get going."

"Thanks for checking out the car. I hope it didn't delay you too much."

"It'll be fine. See you at the end of the term. I'll be praying about that senior project."

"Thanks! Have a safe drive!"

Peter drove away wishing he'd dared to kiss her, while Caroline walked into her house feeling as though he had given her the world. He had said he would see her at the end of the term! That must mean he planned to come home again before summer term started up. It seemed like a long time to wait, but it was the first time he had committed to any definite expectation of seeing her. Best of all, he had said he would be praying for her, or at least for her project!

Spring finally began to creep across the woods, tinging everything in its path green while Caroline watched the progress from above, in her grandmother's third-floor study. She loved the room that radiated her grandmother's sweet personality. This room contained so many of the family keepsakes that had been so important to her grandmother and were now so important to Caroline. She loved the limitless view of the woods and watched with anticipation as the emerging leaves deepened the green mist that gradually unfurled into the undeniable promise of summer.

The skies remained overcast with spring rains and the ground was continually muddy. Cool temperatures prolonged the slow reveal of spring and caused a great deal of low-key grumbling. A sort of universal endurance developed as everyone waited for sunshine and warmer weather. Caroline waited along with everyone else, but she was happier than she had ever been in her life. She had talked with Dr. Calton and he had agreed that her project was worthy of a patent. He also agreed that time was usually of the essence in these cases, but admitted that he had not wanted her to push herself so hard. She began to push herself in earnest. Once again, her life settled into the routine of the life of a true student: she ate, she slept, she studied. And every spare moment, she worked on her senior project that was turning into a full-blown master's thesis. She had little time for other things, but every morning she made time to begin the day with reading her grandmother's Bible, reflecting on the study questions, and talking with the Lord about how to apply it to her life that day. On the rare day when she rushed out of the house without spending time in the Bible, things always seemed to go awry, so she quickly learned that it really did make a difference in her life that she was not willing to risk. She gave Sunday to the Lord as well, making church, Christian friends, and serving others in some way, no matter how small, the priorities for her life. As she learned about the ministries of her church and the importance of giving back a portion of what God gave to her, she began to treat the money she was forced to withdraw from her grandparents' estate as though it were income to herself. She gave a tenth of it to the church because she knew her grandparents' money was God's gift to her for her needs and she wanted to give what she could to those in even greater need than herself. She hoped she would never forget what it felt like to have nothing. She hoped she would never stop being grateful that she had a home of her very own.

Snowdrops and daffodils burst out all along the front

porch, combined with enormous patches of tulips. Caroline watched the flowering shrubs sprout leaves and then swell with sheaves of flower buds until the yard resembled an impressionist painting. Soon forsythia, then familiar lilacs, snowball bushes, bridal's wreath, and many she could not yet identify, decorated the yard with spring scents and sights. She examined the ground daily, looking for signs of new life in the flower beds that flowed around the edges of the house and yard. The lawn company had cleaned out the beds and she rejoiced to see green perennial shoots emerging everywhere. Combing through her grandmother's gardening books improved her ability to identify plants as they shot up, filling the bare spaces. Later, it would be much easier to identify them based on the flowers. In the meantime, she indulged her love of flowers by soaking up their names and descriptions like the black soil soaked up the spring rains.

She had never seen the yard in springtime! Or the summer. She'd only seen the bright golds and purples of autumn when she had arrived at the end of the previous summer. Now, thorny rose bushes began to put out their reddish new growth everywhere around the yard, gradually turning into graceful plants covered in thick, waxy leaves. Grandmother must have loved roses, for they seemed to be represented by a breadth of sizes and shapes. Had she inherited her own love of roses from Grandmother Emily?

On the date deemed safe for planting, she rushed home

from school. She had removed the plastic coverings from the raised vegetable beds and the lawn company had spaded the soft, rich soil. She spent an entire blissful evening poking seeds into dirt along guidelines of straight, taut string. If her garden grew, it would be a thing of beauty.

"Please bless each of these seeds, Lord," she prayed as she made her way down the rows. They had been expensive! She wished she could have afforded more tomato plants, but she would be content with her carefully chosen assortment. She fetched the plants from the greenhouse where they had sheltered for the last week and found it rewarding when she finally stood back to see their leaves mark a simple pattern in one of her raised beds. They looked so inconsequential. Could they really grow into the oversized, sprawling creatures that produced tomatoes?

She worked until sundown, faithfully fastening up the deer and rabbit fence panels around each bed, just as John Lockwood had instructed. They were there, so she might as well use them. Smiling, she remembered the beginner gardening tales of woe that Martha had passed on from her Grandmother Emily. Grandfather Jack had not understood Emily's need to garden, but he had made sure those pesky critters would not get the best of her again. Her grandparents were, no doubt, chuckling their approval at her efforts, from heaven.

"At least my novice gardening attempts have a fighting

chance, thanks to them." Caroline thought that night just before falling asleep. Her collection of seeds were safely in the ground.

Then one gorgeously serene and rainless Saturday, the Christian leadership team from the university came for their end-of-year meeting. They spent the morning finalizing plans for the following year and finished up with prayer, all before lunch. They carried the patio furniture to the back patio and set it out under Caroline's direction and then laid out a "make your own sandwich" buffet on the patio table. After stuffing themselves on thick, meaty sandwiches garnished with everything healthy college students could think of, they cleaned up and headed down to the lake with cans of paint, plastic tarps, and brushes. Drew and Ian carried an extension ladder so that they could reach the highest eaves, and Jeff began to direct the operation.

"Okay. We want to brush all around the edges of the beige walls first so those can dry while we fill in the rest. By the time we've done all of the beige, the edges will be dry enough to paint the white trim right away."

"After that, we get the boats out!" Drew exulted.

"Let's get started!" Mia said, energetically spreading a plastic tarp so it could be taped along the stone foundation. "No paint on the stone or the grass!"

"You guys are amazing," Caroline laughed, comfortable with these students who had become good friends.

Jeff had insisted on providing the paint from an uncle's paint store. After coming to compare a variety of paint chips with the existing paint, he had somehow managed to concoct the color from leftover and returned paint while at home for spring break. Several cans were scattered around the grass, waiting to be used. "Jeff, I still can't believe I'm getting my boathouse painted for free! Please tell your uncle again how grateful I am."

As soon as Jeff had sent Caroline up the tallest ladder to keep her busy painting and out of the way, Mia silently disappeared into the boathouse, as previously arranged.

"I'm going back for the other stepladder," Jeff explained to everyone.

When he returned, all was going according to plan.

"Are we covering it?" Gabbie asked.

Jeff walked around, scanning the surfaces, gave some pointers, and climbed a stepladder to energetically address the mid-level height. Everyone worked hard, and eventually the simple building was covered in new paint. Caroline remained at her latest post, finishing the peak. After surreptitiously checking with Mia, Drew declared it time to take a look at the boats.

"You know I love boating. 'It's the *only* thing!' you know." He continued in a theatrical voice, quoting Ratty from *The Wind in the Willows*, "'Believe me, my young friend, there is *nothing*—absolutely nothing—half so much worth doing as simply messing about in boats.'"

While he posed, Lyndsey painted a white boat shape on the back of his paint shirt and backed away laughing when he turned on her.

"You'll thank me later!" she laughed.

While Drew craned to get a look at his back and chased Lyndsey with his own brush, the rest of the crew began to clean up.

"We'd better get this stuff back up to the house while Gabbie and Ian finish up the last of the trim," Jeff advised.

Lyndsey and Drew helped Jeff and Caroline trek the ladders and paint supplies back to the house. Jeff had set the beige brushes soaking in cans of water, so it didn't take long to clean them and hang them to drip dry.

"To the boats! To the boats!" exclaimed Drew dramatically. "Enough of this landlubberly activity! No more painting!" he declared. But they all knew he had done his fair share of the work and had waited until it was done before yielding to his passion for boats.

They walked good-naturedly down the path to the lake, arriving just as Ian and Gabbie set their white brushes in a can of water to soak.

"I can't believe we did it in one afternoon!" Caroline exclaimed.

"Many hands make short work," Ian smiled. "It looks great!"

141

"It does! I can't thank you all enough!"

Getting the high sign from Mia, Drew offered Caroline his arm.

"This way, m'lady."

"I'm afraid you're going to be disappointed," Caroline warned. "It's only an old rowboat and a canoe."

"Anything that floats will suffice."

"It's not a big lake, but I am excited to get out on it."

Mia stood by the door, grinning. Caroline assumed she had been working on the opposite side of the building and helping with cleanup until she caught sight of the interior back wall covered in a woodsy mural. The curve of a stream flowed toward her, magically blending into the lake water that lapped at the bottom of the wall.

"Oh, my! Who did this? Mia! Did you do this?"

Mia laughed assent.

"Have you been working on this the entire time? It must have taken hours to do this. It's beautiful!" Caroline exclaimed, hugging Mia. "Now I know where you were all that time, and why you all kept me so busy!"

"Aha! You have discovered our great conspiracy!" said Ian with a fiendish look.

"You guys are amazing!"

"It wasn't hard to keep you working," Jeff explained. "Now you know why I was so adamant that everyone stay out of the boathouse until the painting was done."

"I wondered why you kept sending me up that tall ladder!"

"You didn't mind, did you? You don't seem to be afraid of heights."

"No, it was fine," laughed Caroline.

"Pardon me, ladies, but it is time to get these boats out and see if they are seaworthy," Drew insisted.

"By all means! Let's see if these lifts work."

The rowboat and a vintage wood canoe were soon floating in the shallow water, noses to the shore.

"Caroline, I suppose I should tell you that your canoe is worth several thousand dollars. If I were a cad, I would have offered to buy it for fifty dollars, but instead, I'll offer to come over this summer and *professionally* refinish it for you."

"Drew! Really?"

"Yes, really! Who wants a canoe ride?" he asked, paddle in hand. "This work of art is going once around the lake and then we're taking it out of the water to dry thoroughly before it gets a makeover."

"Are you talking about you or the canoe?" teased Lyndsey.

"I'm coming! Don't forget the cookies, Lyndsey!" Ian said, splashing into the canoe.

"Hey! No water in the canoe!" exclaimed Drew. "Make room for Caroline. The owner gets first dibs!"

As Drew continually affirmed, the canoe was a beauty, and his expert handling of the canoe took them serenely across the water. Caroline thoroughly enjoyed seeing the entire lake and the shoreline from the vantage point of the lake as they made their way counterclockwise around the circumference, but she was totally surprised by the undersized dock they discovered a quarter of the way around, on the north side.

"Is that a neighbor's?" asked Lyndsey.

"No, I own all of this side of the lake. I guess it's mine."

"Really, Caroline. You don't know you own a vintage wood canoe worth thousands and you don't know you own two docks on this amazing lake?"

Caroline laughed. "I haven't had a summer to explore. I've been pretty busy. Thanks for painting and getting the boats out. This is great!" As they continued around the west side of the lake, she pointed out the fence coming down to the waterline, separating her part of the lake from the Lockwoods'. "That must be my property line."

"Always a good thing to know," observed Drew.

Lyndsey attempted to smack him with a seat cushion, but he easily dodged the swipe, carefully lifting the paddle and shaking water into Lyndsey's lap.

"Don't rock the boat, *Lynds*," Drew said. "Caroline doesn't want to get dumped in her lake!"

This time, Lyndsey *threw* the cushion at him. It bounced

harmlessly off of Drew back into the canoe.

Caroline didn't mind the teasing that camouflaged such hearts of gold. She had grown to recognize and appreciate that every person in this group was rather special.

Meanwhile, Jeff rowed the rowboat to the center of the lake. Eventually, Drew was convinced to take a second and third trip around the lake so everyone got to experience the canoe before he insisted on lifting it from the water and carefully placing it back in the boathouse.

"I don't know if I'll ever be able to handle the canoe, Drew," Caroline said.

"I'll give you some lessons. What you really need is a kayak so you can get out on your own," he advised Caroline.

"I don't think I can afford a kayak. Besides, I'd probably end up upside down. I think I'll start with the rowboat!" she laughed.

"They aren't that expensive, but you're right, the rowboat is probably your safest bet. I actually examined it earlier, and it seems to be watertight."

"Oh, really?" quizzed Lyndsey. "What would you know about it?"

Caroline laughed, having heard his and Lyndsey's tales of water skiing and boating on the much larger lake near their hometown. Drew had restored several old boats with his dad.

"Thanks for making sure my rowboat didn't end up at the bottom of the lake."

Reluctant but tired, the group cleaned up the last evidences of their presence and dispersed to concentrate on their coursework in a diversity of majors. Caroline reflected on how differently but how wonderfully God had gifted each of them. She was grateful for their friendship. She was grateful for who they were.

With the end of the school year careening toward her, she had no more time for boating. The old rowboat remained tied to the dock, rocking gently, as she concentrated on finishing the year.

CHAPTER EIGHT

Two weeks after the boathouse painting party, on yet another bright, warm Saturday morning, being thoroughly tired of studying and completely finished with classes and coursework, Caroline pulled on rain boots in case of mud and set out along the fence line with a simple picnic lunch in her pockets and a water bottle on a strap around her shoulder. She wanted to be unencumbered and free to explore as much as she chose. Before walking the fence line, she couldn't resist a tour of her vegetable beds bursting with rows of green seedlings. Spring rain and sunshine had coaxed life out of the tiny seeds.

"Thank you, Jesus!" she exulted. "As for you weeds out there, beware! I'll be back!"

Leaving her young garden, she turned north and jogged across the back yard. From there, the sturdy fence struck off straight to the west into the woods behind the house, and Caroline followed, sticking as close to it as she could. She had barely started her explorations before startling two alert

147

does and three skittish fawns. Their flight was instant and complete. So graceful!

Her grandfather had characteristically fenced the entire acreage with a six-foot-high post and rail fence of not just two or three, but four rails. The deer had fled to the interior of her property, into the thickest woods, but she wondered if they could jump the fence at will from a standing position. It was really rather high. She didn't think a horse would attempt it, especially without a running start, something the undergrowth would make nearly impossible. Should she buy a horse?

"A horse's appetite would probably help with some of this tangle," she said out loud, struggling through a thick group of bushes, "but it wouldn't help my pocketbook." Since there was no fence between the house and the woods, a horse couldn't really be contained without additional fencing, and there was no barn. There was no way she could afford new fencing and a barn. The thought of caring for a horse through the winter months was not appealing either, but she wished she had one today. She'd never ridden a horse. The one memory she had of being led around a pony ring didn't really count, except that the person leading the pony had been her mother. It was a nice memory.

Perhaps it would be just as difficult to ride through thick woods as it was to walk through. She skirted the thickest growth, easily finding her way back to the fence because someone, presumably her grandfather or someone who predated him, had planted a mix of evergreens that wound in and out, roughly following the fence line. Scattered groupings of mature spruce invited her to run her fingers over the abundant new growth sprouting in every direction. So soft! It looked as though the fence line had originally been cleared, perhaps when it was first built, but it was filled with shorter growth now. In the more open areas near the fence, the first pink buds of wild rose were beginning to form and would soon scatter their fragrance on the wind.

Occasionally, for a short distance, a narrow path or deer trail made things a little easier before suddenly taking off in another direction. Sometimes, she followed a path into the shade of the evergreens just for fun, but what often looked like a path seemed to meander here and there without reason and sometimes disappeared. It only added to the adventure. She could always find her way back, and the entire glorious day was hers! The birds were audibly celebrating the approach of full-on summer with her, and squirrels were busily twitching bushy tails, then darting off on their business. Being alive was a blessing from God and Caroline was happy to be part of it all. She sang because she couldn't help but sing.

When she arrived at the corner, her wood fence took a ninety-degree left turn to the south, but a barbed wire fence continued in a straight line. There was nothing in sight. The woods extended as far as she could see. As she followed her grandfather's solidly-built fence, the ground began to rise gradually, then more steeply. It was uphill now, and she found herself winding upward beneath tall, straight pines. She could see maples and oaks interspersed with the pines and growing densely down the slope to the east. Somewhere beyond them lay the lake, and beyond that, the house, but she could see neither. She continued easily uphill, tall pines and deciduous trees soaring into the sky around her. When she felt a slight decline begin, she turned back to the highest point and struck out away from the fence, wondering if she might be able to see the house from there.

    She found herself on a high point of land that opened out into a clearing with only a few scattered trees. Best of all, there was a rock outcropping that lined the edge of the hill. What a beautiful spot! She caught just a glimmer of lake water through the trees, but could see no sign of the house or boathouse because of the dense trees surrounding the clearing. Was that just a flash of sun off the windows of her grandmother's third-floor retreat? She searched the woods carefully, but could see no further sign of civilization.

    What a perfect place for lunch! She found a comfortable seat on the rock and spread out her lunch with a feeling of being entirely safe tucked in the woods up here on her own land. She still couldn't believe this was all hers! She loved being outdoors, but best of all, she loved being alone with God.

"Thank you, God! Thank you for the peaceful beauty of this place. Thank you for helping me finish the school year. Thank you for the sunshine and the woods and the lake and everything! Bless my food. Keep me safe. Bless my lunch with your presence, Jesus. Amen."

Caroline ate slowly, savoring the tastes, the smells, the sun's warmth on her arms and back. What a beautiful world God had made! She felt as though she was on holy ground, as Moses had been. She felt God's presence and blessing. How kind God was!

She lifted her face to the sun and basked in the knowledge that she had three weeks before summer term began and she would only be taking three classes. She had pushed for those classes, requesting one of them to count for a requirement that would not be offered until next winter. Now she was on track to be a senior when school began in the fall. She would graduate one year from now at the age of twenty-one, as she had hoped.

She smiled into the sunshine.

"Thank you, God."

When her food was gone and the sun was becoming uncomfortably warm, she took one last peek through the trees before retracing her steps to the fence. The woods didn't seem quite so thick as she followed the next ninety-degree turn of the fence. She was now on the border between her property and the Lockwoods' and her progress was slightly faster as she followed the slope down to the lake. The trees thinned out, but as she neared the end of the fence that she had identified from the canoe, the ground became wetter and she eventually decided to begin circling the lake in a clockwise direction. She wanted to check out that other dock on her way back to the house.

It was slow going, following game trails in and out of miniature inlets while trying to avoid marshy ground. The Lockwoods had told her that the clarity of the water and health of the lake were due to it being spring fed. Even the marshes seemed clean and sandy. Grandpa John had told her that somewhere on the Lockwoods' side of the lake, there was an outlet that allowed a small amount of overflow water to escape. She could look across the lake now and see the Lockwoods' large inlet where she had first skated on the lake. As she made her way carefully around the lake glancing frequently across the water, she eventually saw her own newly-painted boathouse and the path leading up to the house. From the shoreline, the third-story windows of her grandmother's study were clearly visible.

She had lost track of her progress when she suddenly came upon the clearing surrounding the newly-discovered dock. The ground was firm here, and the shore a sandy beach, just like the one by the boathouse. When she walked out on the small-scale dock, the lake depth looked sufficient to bring in the canoe or rowboat. The dock itself was solid. It would be fun to row over and have a picnic, but there didn't seem to be anything here in the open area. Maybe a picnic table would help. Or a gazebo! It would take a great deal of effort to get the materials out here, but it would turn an empty slate into a secluded retreat. She thought of that perfect spot on the edge of the lawn near the house where she had promised herself she would one day put a gazebo. Would two gazebos be over the top?

She wondered, too, if there might be an easier way to get back to the hill where she'd had her lunch. If she could find a path up from the lake that would be nice, but she hadn't seen anything promising on her way around.

There was a path here, leading north, away from the dock into the woods. She might as well explore!

She had hardly started out when she was halted rather abruptly by a stubbed toe. There, nearly buried in the grass, was a ring of stones surrounding a firepit. Perhaps her mother and her family had come here for picnics! Or maybe they had intended to come here. They had always been busy with other activities, and her grandfather had been gone on business so much of the time. Caroline headed away from the lake, following what must have once been a broad swath cut through the woods. She took the time for short jaunts to explore the ferns and violets growing more and more thickly under the trees, stopping to examine unfurling fern tips, lingering to savor the sweet scents. Wildflowers seemed rampantly mixed everywhere with ferns and ivy. Her progress was slow, following clumps of living beauty that lured her under the trees and back out again from side to side along the path.

"God, you truly are amazing! Thank you!"

Caroline stood still trying to take it all in, awed by the delicate beauty of her surroundings. If she could find a decent path from here back to the house, maybe she could pick a wildflower bouquet and get it home before it wilted. The ferns and ivy would no doubt survive. Even their simple woodsy beauty would add life to the breakfast table or kitchen. As she continued, the ground began to slant downward and she made her way back to the path, realizing it led into a large natural bowl densely covered with ferns but free of trees. This was truly spectacular! Wood violets and other flowers were mixed with a variety of ferns. It looked for all the world like an oversized natural rock garden sweeping to her right and to the left, surrounding a natural depression. The path at her feet descended into the lush, low growth where, here and there, angular rocks relieved the vibrant green with their rustic colors. As she lifted her eyes, searching the opposite hillside, she began to laugh.

"What in the world!"

There, directly across the opening, where the ground began to rise on the other side, stood a cottage on stilts. It was somewhat camouflaged in the trees that surrounded it and also by the natural cedar shingles that covered the roof and walls, causing it to blend in with its surroundings. Even the windows were covered by wood shutters that muted the overall appearance, but there was no mistaking its elaborate construction.

"It couldn't be Uncle Brad's tree house! No wonder Grandmother was concerned."

Caroline remembered reading in her grandmother's journal about the time when Uncle Brad had asked for a tree house and Grandfather's response had been to hire a team of workers to construct it while he was on an extended business trip out of the country. Her grandmother had wished instead for something simpler that Grandfather and Uncle Brad could work on together, wisely seeing what an opportunity it could have been for Grandfather to develop a camaraderie with his son. But instead, Grandfather had responded true to character and similar to his other decisions regarding his family. More money and less relationship had been his pattern throughout his life until he finally had nothing left that had truly mattered to him. If only he had turned to God earlier, what a difference it would have made.

Had Uncle Brad played here? Had her mother? Children could have a lot of fun with this tree house even if there was so much that had *not* been left to the imagination. If left to their own devices, she was sure that children would still imagine pirate adventures and, surely, Robin Hood adventures! Mountain climbing. Zorro! Livingstone, I presume? Caroline grinned and examined the steep roof, arched wooden door, and the Gothic arched windows that gave it a storybook appearance and appealed to Caroline's sense of fun. There was even a tower.

As she ran down the path into the basin's natural depression, the tree house loomed above her. Stone steps led up the hillside, but they brought her only to the point of standing under the tree house deck, finding no way up. A pole had been installed at one end of the deck for rapid descent. In spite of her athleticism, it wasn't something she wanted to try shimmying up.

"Looks like a real fireman's pole. It must be ten feet tall."

When she walked around to the back, she spotted a ladder reposing on the deck, safely drawn up to keep out intruders. The distance up to the deck was less here because of the rising hillside. If she could bring a stepladder out from the house, she could easily pull herself up.

"Well, Lord, is there some way for me to get in without going back for a ladder?"

She surveyed the area to see if any of the nearby trees would help, but nothing looked promising. Under the deck again, she spotted spikes set into one of the support posts. It looked like there might be a trapdoor cut through the deck above it. Caroline couldn't quite reach a handhold that would allow her to pull her foot up to the bottom spike, but she managed to haul a log down the hill from the woods and lean it against the post, enabling her to grab a spike and hoist herself up. A few more spikes, and she was pushing against what looked like a rectangular trapdoor above her head. If it wasn't, or if it was fastened down from the top, she would be out of luck. She propped herself against the post and gave an enormous push. The trapdoor swung upward so suddenly and so easily and settled, wide open, on the deck with such a bang that she almost fell off the post. Clutching the spikes and then the edges of the opening, she was able to pull herself up onto the deck.

"Wow!"

She looked around with interest. The deck was littered with old leaves and twigs but not much else. A walk around the perimeter didn't reveal much more than she had seen from below, but there had no doubt once been a clear line of sight from the front straight to the lake and dock. Pirate adventures indeed! Uncle Brad must have had a lot of fun staving off invasions. She couldn't help but wonder what kind of view the tower had.

The arched, wooden door seemed to be the only entry point. It was sturdy and locked. There was also a padlock as an extra measure of protection. More keys to find! She'd found the key to the glass cabinet containing her grandmother's journal in her grandmother's bedside table. She'd found the keys to the MG in her grandfather's bedside stand. Where would she find these keys? She hoped they hadn't been lost or mixed in with other old keys over the years. Hopefully, the locks had done their work and protected whatever was inside.

The shutters were all securely fastened, apparently from the inside. She couldn't even peek in to see what it was like! There was no point in staying. She'd have to come back with keys or break in.

"Let's see what this ladder is all about. Maybe I can lower it so I can get up here more easily next time."

With a little effort she was able to slide it over the edge and lodge it firmly in place.

"Yay!"

She closed the trapdoor, noticing that it had a latch to prevent its use, but she decided to leave it accessible just in case the ladder fell down before she returned. Making her way down the ladder, she hurried back toward the lake, only pausing to gather an armful of ferns and ivy and an occasional flower she couldn't resist.

The path around the lake that led from the newly-discovered dock back toward the house was overgrown but broad and easy to walk. She hurried along, anxious to find the key before the day was finished. She was amused to find that the broad path brought her right to the larger dock and boathouse. If she had known it was there, she could have easily followed it to the smaller dock. She stopped briefly to pick wildflowers to add to her collection. Perhaps all of these flowers had been sown here on purpose, she reflected, looking into the woods to the side where fewer flowers were visible. She was overjoyed with the beauty of her hastily-gathered bouquet.

"I'd better take care of these first," she told herself, entering the door of her flower room. She chose a couple of vases and set about arranging her woodsy, spring bouquets. When she liked the results she texted pictures to Jo, explaining that she had been exploring the woods, and then placed the smaller, more colorful arrangement on the glass top of her white wicker table in the breakfast room. She wasn't sure where she wanted the larger one of fern and ivy, so she left it on the counter of the flower room and ran upstairs. After scouring Uncle Brad's room, she had quite the collection of keys to try! She added a few from her grandfather's study and the kitchen, just in case, and was about to fly out the door when she realized she was thirsty, and probably hungry, too. She was halfway through a tall glass of water when the doorbell rang.

"Ohhhh! Who could that be?"

She knew Jo was busy with her mom today, with Jo's college graduation coming tomorrow, and she wasn't expecting any of the Christian leadership team from school. The Lockwoods were at Grandma Martha's sister's house today. A quick peek through the peephole would tell her if she needed to open the door. She would just wait until whoever it was went away and then she could go check out the tree house.

"Peter!" she said swinging the door open wide. "Peter, I'm so glad you're here! I'm having the grandest adventure!"

Peter loved it when her eyes sparkled.

"What kind of adventure?"

"I found my Uncle Brad's tree house! It's more like a cottage on stilts. Anyway, it's all locked up and I was just about to go try some keys to see if I can get in. Do you have time to come with me?"

"Sure! Sounds like fun!"

"Come in. We'll go out the back door. I was just going to eat a slice of cold pizza. Isn't that terrible? Would you like some?"

"Sure! I happen to like cold pizza. What kind?"

"Mushroom and black olive with tomato sauce and lots of mozzarella. I made it last night, so there's plenty left over. I can warm it in the microwave."

"I'll take it cold. Sounds good! I've been driving all afternoon."

"And I've been tramping through the woods all day! I've been wanting to follow the property line and finally today I had time to do it. It was wonderful!"

They sat at the kitchen table and devoured her homemade pizza and a bowl of mini carrots while Caroline explained what she'd been doing all day.

"And the tree house! You should see it! Over the top!"

She described the setting, the structure, and how she had managed to gain access to the deck.

"Do you think you have the right keys?"

"I don't know, but I collected all of the ones I could find, so I hope so."

"Let's go see!"

As they went through the flower room, Peter commented on the huge bouquet.

"Oh, I forgot! I'll have to find a place for that later."

"It looks like it belongs here."

"You're right! It does!"

As they hurried down the hill toward the lake, Peter noticed the vegetables sprouting in the raised beds.

"You've been busy!"

"Oh, yes! Pray that they grow. It would be a shame if I had nothing to show for it. Not that I know what I'm doing or anything."

"It looks like you did a good job. What all have you planted?"

As they walked down the path, Caroline pointed out the variety of greens and vegetables she had planted.

"Shall we take the path around the lake or row over in the rowboat?" she asked.

"I'm up for a row if you are."

"We can't take the canoe. Drew's going to come over and

refinish it. He says it's worth thousands, and I had no idea. But he says I should keep it and enjoy it."

Drew! Who is Drew? "Wow! The boathouse looks great. Did you paint it yourself?"

"No. The whole Christian leadership team from the university came and did it. Jeff got free paint from his uncle and we all worked on it together."

Jeff! Who is Jeff?

"I brought the key so I could show you what they did to the inside to surprise me. It's amazing!"

Who did the inside? Did what?

"There, see the back wall?" Caroline said, switching on the powerful lights. "Mia did it. Isn't it amazing?"

"Yeah, it looks great!" *At least this one is a girl!*

"And there's the canoe. I think Drew and Lyndsey are planning to start on it next weekend."

Drew and Lyndsey. That's better. But what about Jeff? Jeff and Mia?

"Here are the oars. The boat's tied to the dock now. Jeff rowed it out after we painted the boathouse and Drew paddled the canoe. That's when I discovered the other dock."

"Other dock?"

"Yeah. It's a quarter of the way around to the right. On the north side of the lake. It's right in front of the tree house but you don't notice the tree house because it's set back in the woods and it kind of blends in."

Peter had never seen Caroline so talkative. He was enjoying it. Besides, he needed to catch up with what was going on in her life. *What and who.*

"Thanks for rowing," Caroline said once they were out on the water.

"Sure! I haven't been out in a rowboat for years."

"Isn't it great? I love being on the lake. I know the rowboat doesn't make very fast progress, but I enjoy the peace and quiet. And the slower pace."

"A good break from studying?" Peter asked.

"Exactly. So how long will you be home?"

"I start teaching in two weeks. I've been outlining the courses and brought some work to do while I'm here, so I can spare a few days at least." He didn't want to say that now that he was here with Caroline, he thought he might stay a week. He really couldn't afford that kind of time away from preparing his courses. A lot was riding on his performance this summer.

"Great! Okay, see the dock over there?"

"I see it!" Peter replied with a smile, adjusting his course slightly.

The boat was soon tied up and they began the walk to the tree house. Caroline pointed out the wildflowers, naming the ones she could.

"How do you know so many of them?" Peter asked.

"Grandmother had a book of wildflowers I've been

studying. Isn't it wonderful that God invented flowers?"

"It is!" He was grateful for anything that made Caroline happy.

When they reached the natural bowl surrounded by rocks and trees, Peter stopped.

"I would never have guessed this was here!"

"Me either! See the tree house?"

"Yes! It looks very interesting. But I'm just astounded by the setting. I don't think there is anything like this on my grandparents' property."

"I've never seen anything like it," Caroline agreed. "If fairies were real, I think they would be hanging out here."

"Ha! I think you're right!"

They watched stray sunbeams leaking through the tree canopy and lighting up the lush vegetation.

"I wonder if there is some natural water source watering this indentation from below," Peter speculated.

"That would explain the thick growth of ferns and flowers. I love the rocks and the irregular round shape surrounded by so many trees. The ground is covered with moss, too. Let's go see the tree house. I can't wait to get inside!"

Caroline led the way to the ladder and scurried up.

"I'll have to bring a broom to sweep this deck."

"You've got some moss growing here, too."

Peter held the keys she'd found in Uncle Brad's room

while she tried the ones on the same key ring as the greenhouse, garage, shed, and boathouse.

"I've been wondering what these last two unidentified keys belonged to!" she exclaimed as she successfully unlocked the door.

"I think these two from your uncle's room might be duplicates. Let's see."

"They are! Wow! That's great! I'm glad you noticed. I wonder what all of those other keys of Uncle Brad's unlock."

"Who knows! Boys collect keys. They might not open anything."

They stood in the doorway, leaning into the dark interior.

"My eyes are having a hard time adjusting," Caroline commented.

Peter shone his phone light into the room but it did little to dispel the dusty darkness. Caroline stepped gingerly through the door, shining her light around her feet.

"Let's see if we can get these windows open," Peter said, walking up to one. "It looks like there's a latch on the shutters from the inside." He raised the sash far enough to reach out and release the heavy wooden shutters covering the window. "It's quite the fortress! Look! Each window has a screen that can be pulled down when the window's open, so you won't have to worry about mosquitoes and flies."

With light spilling inside, they easily released the shutters on all of the windows, two on the front looking out to the fern-filled bowl with the path leading to the lake, and two on the back that looked toward the wooded hillside. Peter stepped back out on the deck and fastened the shutters against the walls while Caroline looked around. In the center of the main room there was a wood table with benches, each made of a thick slab of colorful natural wood.

"I'll open the windows in the next room," she said, making her way through an open doorway into what turned out to be a bunk bed room. She walked past the bunks on each side of the room and opened the windows, just as they had in the main room. Peter fastened the shutters back to the sides of the windows on the outside as Caroline looked around. The wall at the end of the tree house sported a long row of hooks and a plain wooden chest beneath the hooks.

"I wonder what's in here. It looks safe." She lifted the lid a few inches and waited in case it should be infested with mice, or something worse.

Let's see!" Peter grinned, rejoining her and lifting the other end of the lid.

"Oh, look! Uncle Brad's dress-up clothes! He must have had a lot of fun with these!"

They pulled out superhero costumes, a doctor's white coat and bag with a real stethoscope inside, and a red fireman's coat and boots with a fire hat that Peter donned. It perched on top of his head, too small to settle properly. When they came across a coonskin hat he added that on top of the fireman's hat. A pirate hat soon joined the menagerie on Peter's head, followed by a space helmet that just fit over the crown of the pirate hat, but it all fell into the trunk the instant he leaned over, causing Caroline to laugh.

"Thank you! Maybe that will scare any mice away," she said. They were nearing the bottom of the deep chest, finding a variety of coats, capes, bags, and cases. Peter picked up a magnifying glass and stared with one wide eye at Caroline, making her laugh again.

"Aha! I've discovered a very beautiful young lady!" he exclaimed, moving closer.

"I don't really want to find the mice. Let's see what's in the other room," Caroline countered.

"You would interrupt a great explorer at his work?"

Caroline laughed and began scooping everything back into the case, coughing at the dust. "I'll have to wash all this stuff," she remarked, wrinkling her nose.

"You'll destroy the evidence, confuse the archaeological layers before I can astound the scientific community!"

Laughing, they made their way back through the main room to the open doorway on the other side.

"I wonder how we climb up into the tower," Caroline said, looking up to the center of the room where the ceiling opened into a second-story level.

"Here's the ladder." Peter indicated the wood rungs built into the wall to the right of the doorway.

"Another trapdoor! This one's easier to deal with. At least it's fastened open."

Peter climbed quickly and helped Caroline through the square hole at the top of the ladder. He had to crouch to keep from banging his head, but Caroline could stand and easily walked around the circular railing lining the larger hole in the middle of the floor. A telescope pointed toward the shuttered window and a ship's wheel was centered beneath it.

"This is quite the tree house. I think your Uncle Brad was one lucky little guy."

"Not really. He had this but he didn't have his father. Grandfather Jack was always gone and when he was home, he was badgering Brad to 'be a man' and forbidding him to go to church."

"Really? Wow, I didn't know."

"Yeah, there was a lot of substance abuse in Uncle Brad's life because of all that. You know my grandfather was delivered from alcohol when he gave his life to Jesus. I wonder if Uncle Brad was lonely here. I don't know if he had friends to bring out here or if he just had Grandma Emily and my mom when he was a kid. Anyway, God protected me from all of that. Here's a rope ladder!" she exclaimed, unrolling it and lowering it over the railing. "What fun!"

"Let's not try that until I've had a look at it to see if it's still sound."

"I thought you were the great explorer!"

"Yeah, well, it probably won't support my weight, and I wouldn't want you to try it until I've examined it. Let's see if I can open this window so we can try out the telescope," he said, lifting the sash and unfastening the shutter. "I'll go down and see if there's a way to climb up and fasten the shutters back."

"You could use the big ladder down there. It's loose. You can just pull it up on the deck."

"Good idea!"

Caroline pushed the shutters back and looked toward the lake. The trees had probably grown a lot since her uncle had played here as a boy, but she could see a section of the sparkling water and a slice of sky above the path. Peter soon came into sight below, carrying the access ladder.

"This should work." He leaned it against the tree house on one side of the window. "Rapunzel, Rapunzel! Let down your hair!"

"Oh, Fair Sir, I fear you will have to climb up," she replied clasping her hands and batting her eyelashes. "Please rescue me before the dragon returns with the troll and my wicked stepmother!"

"How many people will I have to fight off, anyway?"

"Oh, there are many more." She began ticking them off on her fingers. "The evil prince, the sorcerer, the entire pirate crew…"

"I fear we are doomed, Fair Princess, doomed by a

169

muddled fairy tale," Peter stated, fastening the shutter with a grin.

"Indeed, Fair Sir. But if you are my knight in shining armor, nothing is too difficult for you."

Peter moved the ladder to the other side of the window and began to climb.

"Is there a sleeping beauty in there, by any chance?"

Caroline closed her eyes and began to snore.

"We'll have to get you some help with that sleep apnea. You'll keep the whole castle awake!"

Caroline was surprised in the middle of an energetic snore by a brief, strong kiss on the lips. By the time she had opened her eyes, Peter was descending the ladder like nothing had happened.

"It's getting late. Maybe we should head back," he said, pulling the ladder away from the tree house.

Caroline watched him carry the ladder around the corner in the direction of the hillside. She stepped back and took a quick look through the telescope. It evidently needed some adjustment.

Just like me. I need some time to think. What had just happened? She closed the window and climbed slowly down to the main-floor level. The rest of her tree house discovery would have to wait for another day.

Peter rejoined her as she locked the door, and he followed her to the ladder he had replaced. Neither felt like talking, but it wasn't long before Peter's hand found hers. They walked hand in hand down into the ferns and back out the other side. He helped her into the rowboat, took up the oars, and silently rowed toward the boathouse. She was content with the silence. When he had tied the boat to the dock, they walked hand in hand back to the house.

"I'd better go. No rope ladders until I've tested them!"

"Okay."

And then he was gone. She watched his car leave the cul-de-sac, realizing he had not asked her out. No goodbye kiss. No "See you tomorrow," though she was sure he would be at Jo's graduation the next day.

She sat in her grandmother's study until the sunset darkened into dusk. Her first kiss should have been a slow, romantic caress of the lips but, instead, it had been childish playacting. Had it only been mock romance? Had it meant anything to Peter? He had held her hand.

CHAPTER NINE

The next day, Caroline drove to John and Martha Lockwoods' church as usual, the church that had been her grandmother's church, reflecting on the way that it had truly become *her* church as well. After the morning service, everyone involved in Jo's graduation went their separate ways to grab a quick lunch before congregating at the back of the immense chapel at Wield Christian University. Caroline didn't know what to expect from Peter. She dreaded not knowing how to greet him, having no idea how to act after yesterday; but she was soon in her seat next to the Lockwoods, with only a brief wave to Peter who was seated next to his parents; and commencement began. She had avoided contact with him and didn't watch to see if he returned her greeting.

Jo and her friends led the time of worship. Jo was such a gifted person! Or maybe it was just that she wasn't afraid of anything and once she started something she thought God wanted her to do, she did it with everything she had. It was impossible to be jealous of someone as giving as Jo. Caroline was proud of her, and she was sure all the members of her family were even prouder. A long list of awards included an award of appreciation from her classmates to Jo, and Caroline could feel a responsive burst of pride from every person in their row, including her grandparents' old friends, Sam and Millie Larson, who were seated on her other side. The Larsons claimed joint privilege with the Lockwoods of being Caroline's surrogate grandparents, but she couldn't help but wish her own grandparents could have been there with her. What an immeasurable amount of goodness her grandfather had missed in life by refusing God's love for so long! Numerous other awards were given, and then Matt received a preaching award. No surprise there! It was his sermon at the mission that had helped Caroline understand the depth and breadth of God's love.

After commencement, Caroline hung back to allow Jo's family to be the first to congratulate her. She managed to stay out of the family photos, but Jo soon captured Caroline and included her in all of the photos with her friends. Eventually, everyone made their way to the Berkhardt residence, where Jo's parents had set up a backyard party including an outdoor supper. Jo's mother, Claire, had refused Caroline's offer to help because she knew Caroline would be finishing her own course requirements that week. Claire and Bret were obviously thrilled to give their daughter this celebration. The school colors could be seen everywhere, in streamers and ribbons and flowers and cake. Matt and his parents came, as well as innumerable school and church friends of Jo's. Caroline managed to slip Jo a small gift-wrapped package and enjoyed her exclamations over the bracelet inside. It was so perfect for Jo that Caroline had not thought twice about spending beyond her means and was happy for it.

Caroline made a point of continuing to avoid Peter. It was so obvious to Peter that it nearly broke his resolve. Had he offended her with that kiss? He'd had a late night prayer session with his father the night before, seeking wisdom about what to do, and had decided to drive back to school on Monday. He believed it best that he return to his work rather than spend time alone with Caroline. He simply had no idea where his life was headed. Maybe by the end of the summer, he would have a better idea and something to offer her. He knew she was taking classes through the summer. He and his father had left it with their Heavenly Father, asking for things to be made clear in God's timing.

By the time most of the guests had left, Caroline and Peter had still managed to avoid speaking to one another, but when she began her goodbyes Peter was suddenly at her side.

"How about I come by and give the MG a tune up? I need to drive back to school tomorrow, so this is my only chance."

"Sure! Thanks! You don't have to. It seems to be running well."

"It's probably a good idea. I may not have time to do it again until this fall."

Caroline tried to hide her disappointment. Was he going to stay away all summer? No fairy tales. No adventures.

"Okay."

When Peter arrived at Caroline's, he went right to work on the MG. Caroline stayed to hand him tools, knowing their time was short, silently wondering when he would show up again. He began to describe the course he had developed on business ethics, in collaboration with several local businessmen who had consented to participate in a panel discussion for the class.

"Several of them have agreed to mentor an exceptional student in a summer internship at their businesses. So, I'm overseeing those internships as well. The interns will get credit and experience, and hopefully make some connections that will benefit them in the job market."

Caroline was impressed when she realized how closely he had worked with the businesses in his area over the years. It sounded like he had established some great connections himself.

"What will you do when you get your doctorate? Do you want to go on teaching there in the fall?"

"We'll see," Peter smiled. "They haven't offered me a job. I'd like to teach here at home."

Caroline later replayed his smile and the look in his eyes

until she was disgusted with herself. Reading so much into so little would not bring him home any more often.

※

With Jo gone on a ten-week mission trip and many of the leadership team also graduating or gone for the summer, Caroline decided to do all she could to enjoy her first summer in her new home. It would pass so quickly! Drew and Lyndsey came every day for a week. Caroline put in several hours of sanding with them, growing to appreciate the fine features of her vintage canoe under their tutelage, and when Drew expertly applied varnish that Saturday it was as though the canoe came to life. It was indeed a thing of beauty. She gratefully accepted his unending admonishments about not a drop of water touching this canoe until long after the process was complete. He and Lyndsey would be starting jobs in their hometown on Monday, so the process would become slowed by widely-spaced curings of the varnish. He refused any and all payment for his time, saying that it was a privilege to work on it. Caroline fed them and did what she could to let them know how much she appreciated what they were doing, helping whenever they would allow her to. They all knew it was really the time Drew and Lyndsey had together that was the draw, but Caroline didn't mind. She was glad to be a friend of each, and now that they seemed to be an item, she was happy for them.

She wrote to Jo and received many postcards that she shared with John and Martha every Sunday, continuing to have lunch at their house on a regular basis. Jo's grandparents shared with Caroline all that they heard from Jo as well. Together, they were a fan club for Jo and prayed for her constantly. Caroline found herself praying for Peter as well, asking the Lord to bless his courses and all of his efforts on behalf of his students.

Dr. Calton began to work with her to develop what she needed to file the patent for her work, and her appreciation for his sense of humor and relaxed style of encouragement continued to grow. He and his wife invited students to their house every summer for an occasional spaghetti night, and Caroline looked forward to getting to know them better. As empty nesters, they seemed glad to do what they could for students needing a place to hang out and have a home-cooked meal.

Caroline's garden took off in unexpected ways and amounts. She could hardly keep the zucchini picked, cooked it every way she could think of, and gave it away to anyone who would take it. She plugged in her grandmother's extra freezer in the basement and felt great satisfaction in filling it with neat packages of zucchini bread, a few packages of peas, and several servings of green beans when they finally came into full production. In early summer, she ate fresh spinach and the variety of lettuces she had planted until she craved other food. The freezer contained more frozen spinach than she was likely to use. Fresh spinach was so much better! She watched the green tomatoes grow oh, so slowly and couldn't wait to see them red and juicy. Would it ever happen?

To make sure the summer didn't get away from her, she began to schedule time on the lake, drifting in the rowboat or taking cleaning supplies and picnics to the tree house. She couldn't really convince herself it was merely a tree house and privately called it The Cottage. Peter seemed to be an unfading part of the place even though he was far away. She was glad he had shared her first experiences there and helped turn it into the adventure she wanted rather than a sad memory of the shortcomings of her family. She bought two hammocks, one for the tree house deck and the other one for inside the main room. Both became favorite spots to read, brief as her reading time was.

She never tired of deer sightings, of their wariness, their dark eyes, the springs they seemed to have in their feet. The woods surrounding the lake were filled with birdsong, and she actually spotted decent-sized fish from the rowboat. She made a mental note to ask Grandpa John about fishing. The daily sunrise and sunset became a part of her, either looking up from weeding the garden or sitting on her grandmother's classic patio furniture on the covered, stone patio across the back of the house. She loved being part of her surroundings.

Peter's comment about how at home her woodsy bouquet looked in the flower room set her in motion. It would be her summer project. At first, she gathered ideas and began looking for wallpaper and paint that would lend itself to ferns and violets and climbing ivy or other woodsy plants. She decided to take her time and only proceed when she was sure of the outcome. A Saturday class in faux painting helped her decide what she liked and didn't like, and browsing through wallpaper books helped her narrow her focus on what the overall effect was that she wanted in the room. She took pictures of the natural bowl-shaped indentation in front of the tree house, focusing on different plants from different angles until she had accumulated a mental picture of what she wanted. She texted several pictures and sketches to Mia along with descriptions of the spring flowers she remembered and got an enthusiastic response.

"The cottage in the background is perfect! The thick ferns and the plants in the foreground: perfect!"

So, one Friday, Mia showed up at her door prepared to stay the weekend and they began working together on making the one large continuous wall in the flower room look like the natural, open "grotto" (as Mia called it) in Caroline's woods. She had not thought of including the tree house in the mural, but when Mia enthusiastically accepted it as part of the plan from the beginning, she realized it was perfect, just like Mia said. The first thing Caroline did when Mia arrived, was to show her the real thing. They took the path as quickly as they could.

At first sight, her friend was struck dumb with wonder. When she found her tongue again, she raved about the cottage and the setting, took some pictures of her own, and cast a vision for Caroline all the way back to the house. Mia immediately roughed out a sketch and, by evening, they had masked off all of the cabinetry and put up a base coat on all of the walls that would serve as the background color for their mural. They stayed up late finalizing the details of the mural and reminiscing about the last school year. Mia was planning to start a master's program in art history at another university in the fall.

At dawn, Caroline was up, anxious to see the final sketch in the light of day. She was studying it when Mia yawned her way down the stairs from the room Caroline had set up as a guest room.

"What do you think?" Mia asked.

"I love it!"

Mia looked it over before giving her opinion. "I was afraid it might look too storybookish but we were careful to avoid that. It's not overdone. I think it fits your house."

"I do, too. And the cottage is so camouflaged, it doesn't take precedence. It just adds substance and character in the background."

"I like the idea of a haze over the cottage, and the leaves that frame it are perfect. You're right, it's almost camouflaged. Otherwise it would be too cutesy."

"When I first found the cottage the windows were shuttered, so it blended into the hillside even more. I couldn't get over the ferns and spring flowers in the grotto."

"Do you still like the stone foundation we gave the cottage?" asked Mia.

"Yes! It's much more picturesque than the stilts. It just blends into the hillside like the stone stairs that are actually there. I love it! I like the trees that frame the cottage and the edges of the basin."

They assembled a wonderful but quick breakfast of moist zucchini bread and yogurt with fruit so that they could get started as soon as possible.

"I really appreciate your help with this, Mia. You've made me see things from a different perspective. It's much better than I could have done on my own."

"Well, we'll see," Mia laughed. "First comes the hard work of transferring it to the wall and making it look like the drawing. Ready to get started?"

They measured and marked off a grid of squares covering the wall and began sketching in the lines of the drawing converted to the larger scale. For lunch, they took sandwiches down to the lake and ate, luxuriously swinging their feet from the dock. It felt good to be outside and free from the pressures of school for the time being.

Mia insisted on critiquing the mural she had put on the back wall of the boathouse and Caroline had trouble convincing her to leave it as it was. She could tell Mia would never be truly satisfied with it, but Caroline liked it exactly the way it was.

"I still can't believe you guys pulled that off. I had no idea what you were up to."

Mia laughed. "I was afraid you would open the door at any second. I had to work so quietly and carefully and not drop anything or make any noises. And then I was afraid you would think I was off somewhere taking it easy."

"I guess I was so focused on getting the boathouse painted, I just wasn't very aware of what everyone else was doing. Jeff was doing a great job of coordinating it, so I let him."

Mia laughed again. "He's not usually that bossy!"

"You're right, but I didn't stop to think about it at the time. It was so nice of him to get the paint and everything. Have you heard from him since school ended?"

"Yes. He's been driving over every Saturday. He's going to be working on his master's at the same school I am."

"Aha! That's great, Mia! We'll miss Jeff this year. His leadership skills have been so good for the team."

"True, but I think Josh will do a good job."

"I think so too. He really knows his Bible. It'll be good

183

for him to take on the role of leader."

"How about you? You seem to have natural leader instincts."

"You think I have leader instincts?"

"Sure. You have good ideas."

Caroline laughed. "Well, having good ideas and leading are two different things."

"But you're good at getting things done. And hospitality."

"I do enjoy having people here. God gave me this incredible place to live and I like to share it with others, especially when it helps people toward salvation or encourages believers."

"Are you dating anyone, Caroline?"

"Ummm…no. I just really want to finish my degree."

"Yeah, I understand. I'm sure God has someone really special for you when the time is right."

"I hope so," Caroline sighed, revealing the loneliness she denied feeling. "You know how it seems to go: the people I'm interested in don't seem to be interested in me. Instead I have to fight off creeps and guys who just don't appeal to me."

"That's how it was with me until this summer with Jeff. I think it's all about timing. I've always prayed for God to protect me from relationships until he brought the right one at the right time."

"You're right. I pray for that, too. It helps that I just plain don't have time. Life is simpler if I just stay focused. I'll be praying for you and Jeff."

"I'll be praying for you and the right timing."

"Thanks," Caroline laughed.

It felt strange to share such personal feelings. Caroline wasn't used to revealing her heart, but as they worked together through the day, they talked of many of life's difficulties and Caroline was comforted by how Mia interpreted her life experiences through the eyes of faith. It was affirming to have close Christian friends like Jo and Mia who could be trusted. Caroline enjoyed taking Mia to church with her on Sunday morning, and when she introduced her to Jo's grandparents, Mia was warmly invited to join them for lunch.

At lunch, Caroline and the Lockwoods exchanged all of Jo's communications, rejoicing in what God was doing, and Mia's interest was genuine. She seemed to enjoy hearing all about Jo's summer mission activities.

"Peter tells me he's enjoying his teaching. He's asked us to pray about the right faculty position this fall," Grandpa John commented.

"I do wish he could work closer to home," Martha stated with obvious longing in her voice.

"That would be nice, wouldn't it?" Caroline agreed. "You must be missing Jo."

"Oh, yes. But, just like their parents, we'd rather they

were happy and independent and doing what God has called them to. We are blessed to have Claire and Bret so close. It has been such a gift from the Lord to know Jo and Peter as they grew up."

As Caroline and Mia put the last touches on the mural that afternoon, Caroline filled Mia in on more of her history with Jo.

"I'm really glad God brought Jo into your life, Caroline. What about Peter? He sounds really interesting," she suggested with a twinkle in her eyes.

Caroline deflected Mia's inquiry. "They have been so blessed by having John and Martha as grandparents. And John and Martha have been so generous to include me."

"Uh-huh…" Mia laughed. "You're blushing."

"I blush easily."

"Uh-huh."

"Okay, does this top coat of glaze go all in one direction? Which direction are we going?"

Mia laughed and allowed the conversation to move on, but the last thing she said as she pulled away in her little Mazda was, "I'll be praying about Peter!" leaving Caroline no chance to respond.

The next morning, Caroline went straight to the mural. She did love it. Who would ever guess that the storybook cottage in the background was actually her uncle's tree house? It was truly a special place. She pushed away thoughts of Peter's first kiss. In spite of the silliness, that kiss had raised the value of the tree house and she would probably think of it every time she walked past the painting. She forced her thoughts to go in another direction.

Their work looked professionally done. The overall effect was good, not cutesy, not trite, just old world charm that fit right in with the kitchen it was next to. In fact, it added to the flavor of the entire house. She was grateful for her grandfather's insistence on the best for her grandmother. Thankfully, the European classic look of their home was fairly timeless, and she loved it! Before rushing out the door to class, she inspected the wall closely and was relieved to find no glitches in the glazing. Now she could use the same process to add details around the other walls in the room. She could see the perfect places for ferns along the countertop and for ivy poking out from the corners. It made her happy.

That evening, she enjoyed her lasagna and salad on the back patio. The woods at the back of the lawn were filled with pleased squirrels and hyper-vocal birds. She held her breath when a doe and fawn stepped onto the edge of the lawn. The doe moved elegantly but cautiously from shrub to shrub, carefully removing the most delicate new growth at the tips of the branches. The fawn followed closely, a joy to behold. God was so good! What a beautiful creation he had given mankind, and how amazing that he had given her this incredible place to observe it. Nature inevitably turned

Caroline's heart toward God and filled a deep need that she had not known was there before. As the doe and fawn moved off, she collected her dishes and decided to end the day on the lake.

She deposited her coursework and a pillow in the rowboat, untied from the dock, and stepped in. It was cooler on the lake, a welcome relief as the day had been quite warm. Once she was some distance from the shore, the bugs diminished and she settled the oars safely before picking up a textbook. With God's peace within and God's peace without, she focused on the studying she needed to accomplish. Then, when the sun began to set, its light fading, she finally closed the book and lay looking up at the sky, searching out the smallest bits of color. She fought off the urge to get up and do something, do anything. She began to pray for Jo, for Peter, for John and Martha, for Peter's parents, for Mia and Jeff, for Drew and Lyndsey, for Josh, and for the team that would be working and praying to restrain evil on their campus as they spread the good news about Jesus. She was glad to be part of it all. Her heart was full as she watched the first stars come out. It was getting late. Ha! Maybe one of these nights she would sleep in the boat!

She was tired by the time the boat was tied at the dock. She would need an anchor if she really wanted to stay on the boat and not have to occasionally row back from the drift toward the outlet on the Lockwoods' side. She put in a few more hours of studying, prepped everything she would need for an efficient morning, and slept deeply until her wake-up time. The sun was shining and it was another glorious summer day!

Classes. Study time in the library. Lunch in the shade by the campus pond while trying to ignore student antics. The welcome coolness of the computer lab for the afternoon. She had reluctantly taken Dr. Calton's offer of a job as assistant in the lab, and was glad now. It didn't pay much, but she enjoyed helping the underclassmen and often, as today, was able to spend hours on her senior project when no one required her help. Summer students in general were not driven to spend too many hours studying, or in the computer lab, so her help was not often required.

That evening, she researched anchors, consulted Drew about both anchors and the seaworthiness of the rowboat without telling him her plan to sleep in it, ordered a mosquito net (in fact several for her hammocks), weeded her garden, harvested green beans and her first tomatoes, ate her garden harvest, worked on her project, and went to bed excited about life. God was so good!

She chose a Friday night in July as her rowboat sleep-out target and began assembling what she would need. Flashlight. Backup flashlight. She tried out the mosquito net and figured out a way to prop it up and secure it around the edges. She let the Lockwoods know her plans as a safety precaution, she thought through how she would spend the time to make the night seem shorter, and she tried different cushions in the rowboat to find the most comfortable positions for sleep.

Drew and Lyndsey showed up to complete the restoration work on the canoe, bringing an anchor with them. Drew attached it to the rowboat, giving Caroline tips on its proper use and function the entire time, and they all went for a row to try it out.

"Now, you're going to need some fishing poles," Drew observed.

"I think my uncle left a couple of really nice ones in his room." There were simpler ones she was more inclined to use, in a corner of the tree house.

On the target Friday, she gladly set aside her studying, made a few trips to the boat with provisions and worked in the garden until just before dark when she launched out. She settled in with a book and her flashlight, along with her water bottle and an apple to munch. When it was truly dark, she put out the flashlight and surveyed her surroundings. The fish rings had stilled and nothing moved on the shoreline. In answer to her prayers, the anchor seemed to be holding as the boat rocked gently. Hopefully the wind would not pick up during the night. When she had listened to the night long enough to reassure herself, she leaned back and focused on the stars. Again, in answer to her prayers, it was a clear night.

She had never seen the stars like this, a thickly populated host of beings who were observing *her*, too bright, too intense to ignore. It was an uncomfortable thought at first.

One of the reasons she had chosen this date was the expected meteor shower. It was supposed to peak later in the night, but she asked the Lord for a sighting before she fell asleep. Could she fall asleep with all of these stars looking on? She made herself comfortable looking in the direction of the expected meteors. There! And there! Another! Caroline grinned and silently thanked the Lord. A long lull was followed by one more "falling star" that appeared so briefly she almost missed it. She fell asleep during the second lull. It had been a long day.

Her first thought when she woke was that she couldn't believe she had slept all night. She lay still, listening to the predawn intensity of the birds welcoming a new day. The fish were not just biting, they were jumping! She should have brought one of those rods. Next time!

She sat up sleepily to look around, leaving the mosquito netting in place. There was no reason to suffer needlessly. What she saw stopped her short. A single-person tent sat on the shore next to her boathouse. Who was *that*?

There was no sign of life. She watched for a while, praying about what to do. Could be Drew. Maybe he had one last thing he had forgotten to do on the canoe. She folded the netting and began to collect and organize her gear, wondering if Drew would think her very odd for spending the night in a rowboat. She nearly giggled, thinking that it was almost as odd as sleeping in a tent so you could get to work on a vintage canoe at daylight. Maybe he had a deadline and needed to be somewhere later. She glanced toward the tent and watched as a figure emerged and gave a tremendous stretch in the early morning light. *Peter!*

CHAPTER TEN

Peter caught sight of her and walked out on the dock shouting, "Ahoy, there! Requesting permission to board!" Then he stood there grinning.

Caroline cupped her hands and shouted back, "No need. Coming ashore!"

How in the world had Peter ended up sleeping in a tent by the boathouse? By the time she got her anchor stowed and had rowed to the dock, he had his sleeping bag rolled and had taken down the tent.

"What are you doing here?" she asked as she bumped the dock and slipped the mooring line over the post.

"Grandma and Grandpa were worried about you."

She didn't know what to say.

He helped her out of the boat and asked, "How was it? Everything okay?"

"Yes. It was wonderful! How about you? I'm sorry you had to sleep in a tent. What time did you arrive?"

"About one."

"Oh, I'm so sorry! I only told them so someone would know where I was."

"I'm glad you did! I'm fine. Slept great!"

"Did you see the meteor shower?"

"I did! I almost woke you up when I got here, but I was pretty sleepy by then, so I assumed you were out there in your boat, safe and sound, and went to bed. Did you see any of the meteors?"

"I did! Just a few! Was it pretty thick at one?"

"Yeah. It was quite a sight! I'm sorry I didn't wake you. Didn't want to scare you."

"It's okay. I got to see some before I fell asleep, and I slept through the night. I didn't know if I would."

"Good!" Peter rubbed his hands over his face. "Grandma and Grandpa promised a hot breakfast for us both. I think Grandma's making blueberry pancakes."

"I normally reserve the word 'awesome' for God, but your grandparents are truly awesome."

"They are, aren't they?" Peter grinned. "Probably *because* of God."

"Think they're up yet?"

"Maybe not."

"I sure could use a shower before breakfast," Caroline stated.

"How about I help you carry your gear up to your house and then I'll come back and get Grandpa's tent back to him. I can grab a quick shower, too, and let them know you're on your way."

"Sounds good! So sorry you slept in a tent." Caroline hurried to gather as much as she could carry, conscious of the baggy pants and top she had slept in. She must look a sight! She could only imagine what night-in-a-rowboat hair looked like. She had not expected company, and certainly had not expected to see Peter waiting on the shore. At least she was decent, having made sure to be in case of emergencies. She had not foreseen this emergency!

"It was fine. Glad to do it," Peter stated truthfully.

"Well, thanks for keeping me safe."

"It looks like you were comfortable."

"I was. You know, I always wondered what it felt like to get rocked to sleep in a boat. Now I know."

"How does it feel?"

"Nice."

They walked in companionable silence the rest of the way up the hill. Peter dropped his burdens at the back door and headed back down to the lake. "See you in a bit!"

Caroline pulled everything into the flower room, then hastily put away as much as she could. She didn't want to leave a pile in front of her new mural, but she hurried to shower and be presentable before John and Martha might be ready for her.

A short time later, Peter stood in his grandparents' open

doorway watching her run across the lawns after his call telling her that Grandma Martha was busy frying pancakes. She ran with a natural athleticism that captivated him. She looked comfortable and innocent and sort of glowing from within, just like she had looked rowing up to the dock after a night alone on the lake. What an amazing girl!

"How was the tent?" Grandpa John asked him.

"Just like old times," Peter smiled. He explained to Caroline, "When I was a kid, I used to sleep out in Grandma and Grandpa's back yard. Fishing at dawn with Grandpa followed by blueberry pancakes."

"So I've intruded on a tradition. Are there fish worth eating in the lake? I've been meaning to ask."

"Not the best for eating at this point," Grandpa John explained. "I've always thought I should restock it with something better. So how was the lake at night?"

Caroline had not expected to be the center of conversation that morning. She had expected to go quietly home and reflect on her experience alone with God, but since it was impossible to resent the Lockwoods, she would just have to overcome her timidity about sharing the experience.

"The stars were so amazing. I mean, the meteors were great, but even before that they seemed so bright. I've never been out at night like that. It was backwards, as if I were one finite little person with all of these brilliant stars looking down at *me*. Sort of a role reversal. It wasn't what I expected."

"I hope the unexpected isn't all bad," Peter commented, obviously referring to his presence.

"I'm learning that the unexpected in life is a gift from God," Caroline bravely replied.

"It does turn out that way, doesn't it?" Peter said, thinking that God had unexpectedly given him a day with Caroline. "I was thinking, there's this lake about an hour away. It's in national forest, no motors allowed, but we could rent a canoe. There's an old resort there where we can get some lunch. Want to go? They used to have the best ice cream!"

"Sure!" She would weed the garden another day.

"Shall we drive the MG like the true convertible it is?"

"Great idea!" She'd never felt safe about driving with the top down when she was alone, thanks to the creep who persisted in calling her "Princess" or "Beautiful," and this was the perfect opportunity.

Peter took the most scenic route he could think of, taking more time than necessary, but the old road wound through the woods beside a river for part of the way, making it entirely worth it. They didn't feel the need for conversation, content to feel the breeze and enjoy glimpses of sunlight glancing off treetops and river.

It was Saturday, and the aging resort was fairly busy after all. They managed to purchase fishing licenses and rented the last available canoe and fishing poles.

"Not the best equipment," Peter commented, "but maybe we can catch something."

Not surprisingly, the fish weren't biting by the time they found a spot. They were content to drift and talk and drowse in the sun until they knew it was time to find some shade. Back at the resort, they ordered hamburgers and happily discovered that the ice cream was still made onsite.

"This is great ice cream," Caroline affirmed.

"Glad you like it. I haven't been here in years. I'd forgotten how good it is. We used to come here when we were kids."

"I wish I'd known you and Jo then. Jo's doing amazing things this summer, isn't she?"

"She is."

"You two have wonderful parents. I guess I'm a little jealous. Of course they did a great job raising the two of you."

"Of course," Peter said with his typical grin.

"But seriously, how did they do it?"

"They prayed a lot."

"I'm sure that's true," Caroline laughed.

"By the way, I think Grandma's inviting Mom and Dad to come to the home church tomorrow. The plan is that we'll all go out for lunch at some new French restaurant Grandma heard about."

"Great, I hadn't planned on everyone knowing that I

spent the night in my rowboat."

Peter couldn't stop laughing, not even when she attempted to steal his ice cream.

───※───

Somehow, when Caroline and the Lockwoods joined Peter and his parents at church the next morning, she found herself sitting next to Peter and then riding with him to lunch. He had driven his car so that he could drive directly back to school.

"I think Caroline might be the reason Peter came home this weekend," observed Claire to her husband as she served as navigator to the new restaurant.

"I think you're right. Last time he was here we had a talk. He was asking for advice because he's quite serious about Caroline."

"I didn't know it had gotten that far."

"He didn't want you to get your hopes up. He's applying for teaching positions here in town. I don't think he's heard from any of them yet."

"Oh, I see!"

"She seems like a lovely young lady," observed Brett.

"She is. She's been good for Jo, and Jo has been good for her. She had a rather tough time growing up without her family."

"Something to pray about."

"Yes. She has become quite a strong believer. She's quite brilliant."

"This is the first time Peter has ever been serious about a girl," Brett reminded her.

"Yes, I think it is. But she is young."

"I get the impression that Peter is willing to wait."

"We'll have to pray for what's best."

After lunch, Peter drove Caroline home but left his car running while he walked her to the door.

"I'm glad you came home this weekend, Peter, but I'm sorry your grandparents thought it was necessary. Sorry about the tent!"

"I'm not sorry. I enjoyed every minute of it." He pulled Caroline toward him, brushed his lips across her forehead, and released her. "See you later."

"Later," she managed to say as he climbed back into his car.

She wished for so much more, but it was useless. She had her life here and Peter had his elsewhere. Becoming a follower of Christ had changed her priorities, but she felt God's call to remain where she was and finish what she had begun. Just as Peter obviously did. Caroline felt her energy drain away as she stepped through her door. She had not slept well Saturday night, not half as well as she had slept in the boat, but once in a rowboat was enough. She and Jo were planning an overnight in the tree house in August when she returned from her summer mission work. Perhaps Peter would show up again. In the meantime, Caroline needed a nap. Right now. She managed to pray for Peter's safe return to school before falling asleep. Poor Peter. He had certainly not had a restful weekend! Not that she was really sorry Grandma and Grandpa Lockwood had felt compelled to inform him. He had, no doubt, come out of respect for them, and he had kept things so casual between them that she wasn't at all sure he had come out of any actual concern for her.

Making good use of the firepit by the tree house, Jo and Caroline carefully turned their marshmallows over the open fire in pursuit of the perfectly golden goo warm enough to melt the chocolate bars.

"I'm really glad we finished our study of John before I left for the summer. I was able to start several of the girls on it there. It was such a blessing to me," Jo began.

"You were in some difficult situations."

"Yes. That's when God did the most miraculous things."

"I think I understand a little bit. Josh and I managed to pull off the movie outreach event for the summer. It wasn't easy, but five people accepted the Lord. I started the study of John from the beginning last week with the three freshman girls who became believers." She left unsaid that she and Josh had ended up covering a large portion of the expenses themselves and that she had purchased Bibles and study guides for the three girls.

"Tell me about Josh," Jo requested with a sinking feeling. Peter had confided to her under the strictest warnings of confidentiality that he had applied for the opening in the computer science department at Caroline's university but it had gone to someone more experienced. Was the Lord telling them all that Peter and Caroline were not meant to be?

"He's a good guy."

"Yeah?"

"Not like that! He's not special to me, Jo, but he does care about getting the good news out to people. He's doing a different study with the two guys who came to the Lord at the movie event."

"Wow! That's really great! It's wonderful what God has done through the leadership team at your university. I'm glad you're part of it."

"Me too! I never thought I'd be doing this."

"I knew you would."

They washed their sticky hands in the lake and put out the fire before heading for the tree house. They had carried everything over earlier that they would need for the night. Jo paused on the edge of the basin.

"I still can't believe this is here. Even in August it's green and fresh. The ground is soft with moss and rotting wood. I love the rocks."

"Isn't it wonderful? Peter thought maybe there's a spring or underground source of water."

"Oh! When did he see it?"

"The day before your graduation. He just happened to come to the door the day I discovered it, so I showed it to him."

"And?"

"He helped me find the right keys to open it up, and then he fastened all of the shutters back to let in the light."

Jo couldn't suppress a smile. So Peter had shared Caroline's first discoveries in the tree house! Funny she hadn't mentioned that before. Neither had Peter!

Caroline pointedly ignored Jo's satisfaction and continued, "I was glad someone was with me. It kept me from being sad or afraid."

"Uh-huh."

"What!"

"Oh nothing!"

Jo laughed. Caroline let her. There was no way she was going to tell Jo about their silliness that day, or about that absurd kiss.

"And then there was the night I slept in the rowboat and when I woke up, Peter was sleeping in a tent on the shore."

"What? I leave town for the summer and you forget to

tell me these minor details? Wait a minute. You slept in your rowboat?"

Caroline laughed. "I did! No one was supposed to know. I told your grandparents just in case of emergency, but they told Peter and he drove half the night to get here to keep me safe!"

"He did?"

"Yes! Of course I was perfectly safe, but it was nice of him to come. I felt sorry that he had to sleep in a tent, but Grandma Martha fixed blueberry pancakes for us. I guess it's a family tradition from when he and Grandpa John would go fishing at dawn."

"Yes! I used to come sometimes when Peter and I were little. It was so much fun! Sometimes I went out in the boat with them and sometimes Grandma and I would have the pancakes all ready when they came in from the lake."

"Tell me more of your family traditions. I don't have memories like that."

Jo sobered instantly. "I'm sorry."

"No! It's okay! Just tell me what it was like growing up in your family. Tell me more."

"Once when we were little, Peter jumped off the top of the slide into a snowbank. I always tried to do everything he did. So, being four years younger, when I tried to jump off the slide into his footprints, I twisted my ankle; but he carried me to the house and told Mom what happened. He felt so bad because I was trying to imitate him. I think he always worried about that from then on. He was so careful to watch out for me."

"What are some of your other favorite memories growing up?"

"I think a lot of my favorite memories are from church. Mom's been teaching a women's Bible study for years, but when we were growing up, she was always in the children's area with us, too. Mom always taught children's Sunday School classes and children's church. She started a children's choir. She was always involved in organizing and teaching the summer events, too. She always had props and teaching materials at home. We used to play with them and learn the Bible stories ourselves, at home. I always loved the stories of the New Testament, but there was something about Abraham that always appealed to my sense of adventure. He lived in places so foreign to us, such a different lifestyle, but he was willing to leave everything familiar to obey God."

"Now I understand how you know the Bible so well. And why you want to be a missionary."

"I suppose. I gave my life to Jesus when I was five years old. I remember it being such a big decision. I felt as though heaven held its breath. As though I'd found the place I fit. I can't explain very well, but I knew I would serve Jesus somewhere else in missionary work."

"Wow, Jo. That's amazing! I didn't have that experience.

I was just flooded with joy! I knew I really belonged to Jesus, so I found my place, too, I guess. I should be willing to go somewhere else, but I feel like my place is here for now."

"God doesn't call everyone to be a missionary in another country. He calls most people to be missionaries where they are, and that's what you're doing. Remember when you asked about Peter and whether he felt called to be a missionary?"

"The day I first met you!"

"Yeah! Peter believes he should use the gifts God has given him to impact the academic and business worlds. He loves the technology side of things, so that's the way he does it."

"He told me a little about how he works with local businessmen, connecting them with his university to help students. I've never heard of anyone doing that."

"That's his special gift. Now that I think about it, he's always involved in bringing people together when he sees how they can be mutually beneficial to each other. And in the process, he always finds a way to tell them about Jesus."

"That's a cool gift."

"It is!"

"Which game shall we play?" asked Caroline, shuffling the stack of games they had brought from the house.

"We carried that heavy Aggravation board all the way here, so let's give it a try."

Jo started music playing on her phone and they read

through the directions as they set up the wood board by placing marbles in the hollows scooped out for them. In addition to the typical board that came with the game, they had found this satiny wood one in Caroline's grandparents' game cupboard. The gleaming wood and its handcrafted uniqueness was what had appealed to them in spite of the fact that neither one of them had played the game before.

They were into their third game when they looked up in surprise.

"Did you hear something?"

"Someone's here!"

They rushed out to the deck railing in time to see Peter poised on the opposite side of the basin with his tent roll on his shoulder.

"Ahoy there! Requesting permission to come aboard!"

"What do you think, Jo?" Caroline shouted. "Should we let him in?"

"I don't know. Party crashers aren't nice. How do you think he found out we were here?"

Peter approached the cottage. "I'm always having to come and rescue you girls! Can't you behave yourselves? Are all young ladies enticed into sleeping in rowboats and tree houses?"

"I didn't tell Grandma and Grandpa," Jo said, shaking her head.

"I didn't either," Caroline chimed in.

"Well, it was Mom and Dad this time," Peter informed them.

"Mom and Dad!"

"Yes."

"Worried about us?" asked Jo.

"Yes."

"I guess we'll have to let him come aboard, then," Caroline grinned, raising her hands in a helpless gesture.

"Ever played Aggravation?" Jo asked him.

"Never!"

"Welcome aboard!" they shouted together.

Caroline and Jo had carefully latched the trapdoor and pulled up the ladder, secure in their castle surrounded by a moat. Of course, it didn't matter now that Peter was there. Caroline ran to lower the ladder.

"Watch the alligators," she instructed as Peter started up.

"Alligators!"

"In the moat!"

Peter tossed his tent onto the deck and then his backpack. "Thanks for the tip," he said with a grin.

The three of them were soon in the throes of a highly competitive game aimed at getting their marbles around the board while sending their opponents' marbles back to the beginning.

"It's midnight!" Jo exclaimed hours later.

"All right, this is our last game," Peter warned. "One

more and I win the championship." In truth, they had lost track of how many games they had played, so when Jo won this one, she claimed the title.

"Thank you very much!" she said, taking a bow. "Aggravation champions of the world, make room for a new member, soon to become World Champion."

"My sister is the champion of aggravation? No comment!" Peter grinned. "Mind if I sleep in the hammock out there?"

"Sure. It might be more comfortable than the hard deck," Caroline agreed.

"Blueberry pancakes in the morning!" he informed them.

"What? Grandma and Grandpa know, too?" Jo asked.

"Sure. I parked my car there. Had to tell them what I was up to and borrow the tent."

"Next time I sleep in the rowboat, I'll just put a notice online so the whole world knows," Caroline said with resignation.

It was difficult to stop the contagious laughter that followed. Peter pulled up the ladder again, declaring that he had no wish to be surprised by alligators during the night. The girls had settled in their bunks and Peter in the hammock slung across a corner of the deck when he called them to come out and see the stars.

"There are a lot of trees, but if you lie down on the deck and look straight up, it's pretty good," he said from the

209

comfort of his hammock.

"Easy for you to say!" Jo teased.

"Psalm 147," Caroline murmured. "He determines the number of the stars and calls them each by name. Great is our Lord and mighty in power; his understanding has no limit."

They spent some time admiring the starry host and praising the Lord for the beauty of his creation before the girls climbed back into their bunks and fell asleep. The next morning, Grandpa John found his way to the tree house to announce that Grandma was making pancakes.

"I guess I never did see this place. I remember when they were building it. Contractors and machinery driving back in here, but I never paid much attention. That uncle of yours was a lucky boy."

"Not so much, Grandpa John. He didn't have family to share it with," Caroline reminded him. "Jo and Peter are the lucky ones. They have you and Grandma Martha!"

"Well, she's going to have those pancakes sizzling, so we'd better get back there and help her out by eating them," he said. Caroline had never seen him embarrassed, but he seemed to be now.

"How was the hammock?" she asked Peter.

"Great! Slept like a baby. No comments from my sister, please!"

"Ughhh. It's too early in the morning for comments." Jo

replied with a yawn. "But, Caroline, you'll have to come stay at our house after Peter leaves so we can have all the girl talk we missed out on last night because he was here."

Caroline merely smiled. She would rather have Peter there than have all the girl talk she could imagine.

CHAPTER ELEVEN

The fall term began with a vengeance. Between the leadership team, her senior project, keeping up with course requirements, and working in the much busier computer lab, she hardly had time to think. And then, there was the new professor.

"Caroline, isn't it?" he asked, catching her alone in the computer lab one morning.

"Yes." She didn't like the way he looked at her. She sent up an immediate prayer for protection. This was not a man to trust, not a man to be alone with.

"I look forward to getting to know you. Would you…"

His sentence was interrupted by the approach of two women students, and his smarmy good looks and charm were turned on them. Caroline made her escape and from then on stood in the hallway until there were students in the room. How would she describe the look in his eyes? Greed? The hunger of an experienced wolf? She couldn't put it into words, but she knew what it meant.

Why hadn't Peter applied for that teaching position? Caroline hadn't known about the opening before it was filled, so maybe he hadn't either. But Peter had defended his dissertation and it was a sure thing now, yet he continued to teach there instead of moving back home. Was there someone there, someone who kept him there?

Her time became stretched to the limit. Busier than ever, with more friends and more responsibilities than ever, she couldn't understand the growing sense of loneliness that followed her through her days. There was a weariness creeping into her heart. The closer she got to her goals, the less sure she was of what she wanted, of what God wanted. Nevertheless, she remained thankful. Her goals were nearly within reach.

Jo was out of town now, excited to be working on a master's degree in missions at a well-known seminary. When she called that evening, she was bubbling over with all that she was learning. She had chosen her seminary carefully, and was thoroughly enjoying the theology, hermeneutics, and New Testament classes in an academically challenging but trustworthy setting.

"Peter's going to walk in his doctoral graduation in December. Mom and Dad are going to drive Grandma and Grandpa, and I'm going to caravan so you can ride with me. We might have some other passengers, but I'm not sure yet. I'll let you know more in December. So how's the new professor?"

"Smarmy."

"Smarmy! What does that mean?"

"I avoid him completely and please pray that it continues to be *completely*."

"That bad?"

"That bad."

"Sorry. So what else is going on?"

"The leadership team came over for our fall meeting last weekend. Things are on track for our next event. I'm going to miss your help with new students." Caroline remembered how empty the house had seemed on Saturday when the team left.

"I'm going to miss that, too. I'm helping with an urban mission here, and I think I'm really going to enjoy it."

"That sounds good. How's Matt?"

"He's fine. He's working with the urban ministry, too, so we'll get to work together a little bit throughout the year."

"That's good. Do you know anyone else there?"

"No, but it's fun to be part of such an amazing student body. It felt that way being in a Christian college, but it's even more that way now."

Caroline was genuinely happy for Jo, but wished she felt more positive about her own life at this point. Everything was great, so why didn't it *feel* like everything was great? She loved everything she was doing. Maybe she was just tired. She looked forward to spending entire days on the lake and in the tree house during Thanksgiving break if it wasn't too cold. Or, maybe she should travel like everyone else, but she didn't know where she would go. She didn't really want to travel alone and there wasn't anyone she wanted to travel with. Anyway, that was weeks away. Until then, she just needed to keep on keeping on.

On Tuesday during the week of Thanksgiving, Peter and Jo showed up at her door. The three of them played Ping-Pong, made pizza, and listened to old CDs from her grandparents' collection.

It was on the way home that Jo said to Peter, "I'm tired of playing chaperon. Why don't you ask her on a date?"

"A date?"

"A date, Peter! A real date. A nice dinner. A movie. Skydiving if you think she would like it, but a date!"

"You're right, Jo. Sorry."

"It's okay. You know Caroline and I are the best of friends but three's a crowd."

"Sorry, I thought we were all just hanging out together."

"You're on your own tomorrow, so you'd better make arrangements, brother. By the way, I'm all in favor."

"In favor?"

"Of you dating Caroline. Grandma and Grandpa and Mom and Dad and everyone else we know are in favor of you dating Caroline."

"What?"

"Just think about it. Flowers, gifts, just the two of you."

Peter grinned all the way home.

The next day, Caroline was astounded to receive a dozen red roses and when Peter called to ask if she would like to go out to dinner that night, she nearly stopped breathing. *A date? Is he asking me on a date?*

"Uh, sure!"

"I'll pick you up at seven."

"Ummm... how should I dress?"

"Not formal, but we'll dress up if that's okay."

"Sure! That's great!" *What in the world will I wear?*

"See you at seven!"

Caroline sat for a minute, overcome by the turn of events and trying to focus on what she needed to do to get ready. What did she have to wear? Something she wore to church might do. After all, she had clothes he had never even seen! But when she frantically paged through her closet, it was far from satisfying. She wanted to look amazing! Maybe she was taking this too seriously. Peter wouldn't take it so seriously would he? "We'll dress up," he'd said. "Not formal, but we'll dress up." Where were they going?

There was that gorgeous silk in her grandmother's sewing room, but she could hardly whip it up in the hours between now and seven tonight, even if she had the right pattern for it, which she didn't. She was going to the mall. She needed a dress.

"Please, Lord, I need your help to find something nice, something not too fancy or expensive, but something nice," she prayed all the way to the mall. "Help me to find the right store and the right dress at the right price."

Two hours later, she promised herself to purchase the perfect pattern for that silk when this was all over. If there was a next time, she wouldn't be caught off guard. Beginning to tire, she walked into a store she had always avoided, thinking it beyond her means. They were having a sale! She tried several dresses, and when she found it, she knew it was the right one. Shoes! Now she just needed the right shoes!

Peter rang the bell promptly at seven and when she saw the look in his eyes, she knew it was the right dress, and the right shoes. She would have happily paid twice the amount to know she looked this good for Peter.

How was I to know she looks like this when she dresses up? Peter was overwhelmed by the beauty of this girl, uh, woman who'd stolen his heart at first sight. He'd have to remember to thank Jo. To think he could have missed this!

They were ushered to a table by the fireside, a table draped with white tablecloths and artfully folded cloth napkins, with fresh flowers in a sparkling glass vase. He held her chair for her and Caroline realized that no one had ever done all of this for her before, not in her entire life. She blinked back tears. Peter! Peter had done all of this! For her!

The food was delicious and the service exceptional. They

had such a good time talking together, it was as though they had been saving up all of their best experiences to share with one another when there was no one else to interfere. Looking into one another's eyes was entirely different tonight than any other time.

When Peter finally left her at her door and said goodnight, he drew her carefully into his arms and kissed her. Really kissed her.

"See you tomorrow," he said. And then he was walking toward his car.

Caroline stepped inside feeling happier than she ever remembered feeling. Peter, handsome, wonderful Peter had taken her out to dinner and kissed her! The scent of roses greeted her from the arrangement she had set on the entry table. No one had ever given her flowers before. Well, no one that mattered! She could hardly sleep, thinking of Thanksgiving Day tomorrow at the Lockwoods.

Jo and Grandma Lockwood conspired to seat Peter and Caroline together, and no one seemed in the least surprised to see them there together, as though it had always been so. When they all joined hands to pray before the meal, Caroline's hand found its home in Peter's. She was glad when Peter reclaimed her hand under the table after the prayer. When the details of attending Peter's graduation were discussed, it was assumed that Caroline would be part of the festivities. He would look so distinguished in his doctoral robes! Was this all real?

"I have to head back tonight," he said in a low voice for her benefit after dinner.

"Tonight?" she asked.

"Yes. I'll call you this weekend?"

"Okay," she smiled her assent.

"I'm sorry, but I have so much to do before classes on Monday."

"I understand."

There were no goodbye kisses in front of the family, only a wave of the hand to everyone, and he was gone. His graduation was two weeks away and she would have her hands full finishing her own term.

"Lord, Peter's life seems to be so bound up with his doctoral degree and where he is," Caroline prayed. "If I need to be willing to give all of this up to join him there, than please help me. This house is yours, Jesus. Thank you for letting me use it, for bringing me here, for all that it has meant to me. Thank you, Jesus, for my wonderful grandmother. Thank you for her journals. Thank you for protecting me for all of these years and for giving me salvation. Jesus, if Peter and I are meant to be together, please work it out. If not, please help me."

Peter's calls had been infrequent and she couldn't help

but feel he was holding back. There was a barrier of some kind. Something was keeping him from committing to her and making plans for the future. Was there someone he was dating there where he was? His teaching seemed to be taking all of his time, but maybe there were things she didn't know. Maybe his heart was really there and not here with her. Their conversations seemed so awkward because they always seemed to be edging around any real commitment. Did he love her or not? He had never said so.

"Lord," Peter prayed, alone in his apartment, "please work it out for me to get a job at home so I can really court Caroline. It's what I want, Lord. It's what I need."

"Lord, please work things out for Peter and Caroline," Jo prayed every day.

"Lord, please bring Peter home if that is your will. Please bless Peter's teaching and please provide a job for him here if you want to bless him in that way. Please work out what's best for Peter and Caroline. Strengthen them and make them into the people you want them to be," Bret and Claire prayed.

"Lord, you know Peter and Caroline want to do what's best. Please help them. Please provide a job here for Peter," prayed Grandma Martha and Grandpa John.

"Hello?" Peter answered his phone. "Yes. Yes, I'm still available. I haven't signed the contract for the next term. Yes, I can come for an interview." Why did it have to be the day after graduation? His entire family was coming and would be

221

staying over at a nearby hotel. He, however, would be driving back that night, immediately after graduation, in order to appear at an early morning interview at Caroline's university. He wondered what had happened to the new hire. Or had someone else left? He wanted to call Caroline. He needed to call Caroline. Tell her what? That he wanted a job at her university so he could date her? Maybe it would be wiser to call his family and ask them to pray.

The week of Peter's graduation, rumors were rampant on Caroline's campus. The new hire was nowhere to be seen. He and the university were named in a lawsuit and he had been dismissed. Several lawsuits, some claimed. Jo told Caroline that Peter had been asked back for an interview. Asked back? Then he had applied for the position before?

"Wouldn't it be wonderful, Caroline?" Jo asked.

"Yes."

"He didn't tell anyone before because he didn't want us all to be disappointed if it didn't work out. It didn't, but maybe this time it will. We're all praying!"

"Me too!"

"There's only one catch. He has to drive back right after the graduation ceremony so he can get to the interview the next morning."

"Are we still going to the graduation?"

"Yes. Mom and Dad don't want to miss it. You'll still come, won't you?"

"Yes. I think so."

"I'm counting on your company on that long drive, and back again the next day."

"I think I can manage it." *Why isn't Peter telling me these things? Why hasn't he called?*

Maybe she didn't mean anything to him after all and she'd been building childish pipedreams out of one date. How could she stand to watch him graduate like she was one of the family, like another sister? How could she watch him be congratulated by his friends, perhaps by someone special to him? Could she stand to see him with someone else? *Help me, Jesus! I can't do this!*

Jo thought Caroline seemed subdued on the Sunday drive to Peter's graduation. Wasn't she happy for him? Wasn't she excited about his interview the next day? Maybe she was just tired from finishing her own term. Jo had finished the week before and was on winter break, but Caroline's schedule was going unusually late this year. In fact, Jo knew Caroline had made arrangements to miss a few things the next morning while they were making the return trip. Most students were gone, and it was potentially Caroline's last day on campus. Maybe there would be news about Peter's job by then!

"Are you okay, Caroline?"

"Yeah, just tired," Caroline answered with a weak smile. She could hardly ask Peter's sister how he felt about her.

There was no time before the graduation ceremony

began. There was Peter, seated in his row of doctoral graduates, and here she was with all of his family, merely looking on. He was stunning in his robes, just as she had known he would be. He seemed happier than she had ever seen him. He waved at them all, and they all settled in for the long ordeal, or at least what seemed like a long ordeal to Caroline. She hardly took her eyes off the back of Peter's head the entire time. She couldn't help but feel proud of him when he received his diploma. She clapped and smiled with tears in her eyes along with everyone in the family, knowing how hard he had worked and how God had gifted and blessed him. How could she stand to see him on campus everyday if his heart belonged to someone else?

Afterward, she congratulated him along with everyone else and gave him a hug like everyone else. There were plenty of other students waiting their turn to talk to him and congratulate him.

"I'm so glad you came, Caroline," was all he had time to say before being pulled aside by fellow students and faculty for more congratulations.

Caroline watched a gorgeous blond give him a long hug, congratulate him, and take a position next to him. Was that who Peter really cared for? She couldn't blame him.

Eventually, he found his way back to his family in order to express regrets about not being able to join them for the dinner they had arranged in his honor.

"I'll let you all know as soon as I know something!" was his cheerful goodbye as he left. He exchanged goodbyes with other students all the way to the door.

"See you later," said the blond perfection, waving at him as he finally reached the door.

They all went rejoicing to dinner, praying silently for his safety on the drive home, and for him to get the job if it was God's will.

"Why does Caroline look so unhappy?" asked Bret.

"She's probably tired, and now the suspense is no doubt getting to her," answered Claire. "So much is riding on this job offer. And Peter had to leave so suddenly. They hardly had opportunity to talk."

"I'm sure he'll call her later," Bret assured her. "We'll have to try to cheer her up."

Caroline convinced Jo that she wanted to turn in early that night in order to be rested for the trip back. They needed to get back in time for her to do her afternoon shift as assistant in the computer lab. Jo was happy to agree. Her parents and grandparents had already called it a night, and she had to drive the next day. Caroline had driven part of the way and would no doubt offer to help with the driving on the way home, but she had been so quiet Jo wondered if she was coming down with the flu like last winter.

The next day, Caroline only had time to exchange her overnight bag for her backpack after Jo dropped her at her house. She was on the road to the university within half an hour, tears streaming down her face. She could not face the future if it included that gorgeous blond or anyone else on Peter's arm as he walked her campus.

"Lord, I can't do this. Help me."

She loved him. She had loved him since she had first opened the door to the computer whiz of a grandson that Grandma Martha had sent to help her out more than a year ago when she had first come to claim her grandparents' home. She loved him so much it would tear her apart to see him with someone else. It was that simple. And she had no reason to believe he returned her feelings.

Peter sat in the office of the university president, grateful for his congratulations on being offered, and accepting, the job. The interviews had gone well and they had kept him busy all day. The job was his! Signed, sealed, and delivered! He had just answered a call from his dad and told him the good news.

"The committee was impressed with you all over again, Peter. I shouldn't tell you this, but it was very close the last time around and we made the wrong choice. I think everyone is excited about your emphasis on ethics in business practices, and very interested in what you've started even in the time since we last talked. Your innovative approach to mentoring and the connections you've created between your university and the local business community are stellar. We look forward to you doing the same here for us. Welcome aboard!"

"Thank you, sir," Peter answered, eagerly returning the president's handshake. "I look forward to doing that. I'm grateful that you see the value in establishing those relationships in the community. I think we'll see benefits for everyone."

"Yes. And, oh Peter, there's just one more thing. You've probably heard the rumors around campus. Anyway, I'm sure the committee filled you in on the current lawsuit and our position. We are sure we can count on your discretion. And with your emphasis in ethics we are relieved."

"Yes, sir. I'm happy to do whatever I can to help."

"So you'll understand when we ask you to honor our new faculty code of conduct, including no dating of undergraduates. Or graduate students for that matter. We don't want any more trouble like what we're dealing with now."

"Yes, sir," Peter replied, barely able to speak. No one had mentioned the new faculty code of conduct.

"Well, I'm sure you have things to do. Looking forward to what you're going to do for us," the president said, holding the door for Peter.

His time with the president was obviously over and so

was his time with Caroline. Peter descended the stairs deep in silent prayer.

"What have I done, Lord? Did I rush in without asking you if it was the right thing to do? Is there someone else that Caroline cares about, someone else you have for her? Have I assumed too much? Forgive me, Lord. Help me to know what to do."

He wondered if Dr. Calton was in his office. He didn't know who else he could talk to and he had to talk to someone. He absentmindedly opened the door to Dr. Calton's building and stepped aside to let someone exit. Caroline!

"Peter! How did it go? Did you get the job?"

"Ah… Miss Engbert. So nice to see you."

Miss Engbert! So nice to see you? Caroline stood baffled as Peter entered the building without a backward glance. So that was the way it was! There was someone else. She couldn't do this. She couldn't be just another undergraduate student welcoming the new professor, pretending they were strangers. If he had gotten the job, she would have to sell her grandparents' home and move to another state.

"Dr. Calton?" Peter said, tapping on the partially open door. "Do you have a minute?"

"Sure, Peter! Come in! I understand that congratulations are in order."

"Yes. Thank you, but there's a complication, something I just found out about."

"Oh?"

"Yes. Uh, you see, I've already accepted the teaching position, but I didn't know about the new faculty code of conduct."

"I'm not sure I do either. What's in it?"

"Uh, no dating undergraduates or graduate students."

"Is that a problem?"

"Do you know Caroline Engbert?"

"Oh, I see! So that's the way it is."

"That's the way it is. She's the reason I took this job."

"I see." They sat in silence for a moment. "Have you talked to her about it?"

"No. I just found out about it."

"So, you're dating."

"Yes, I mean I was hoping… "

"Hoping what?"

"Hoping to spend my life with her."

"Have you proposed?"

"No. I guess it's fortunate that I haven't."

"Fortunate! I don't think anyone could object if you were married."

"Married?"

"Yes. They can't keep you from marrying her! In fact, they'd probably be happy if you were a married man."

"But she's so young. I thought I should wait."

"How old are you, Peter?"

229

"Twenty-seven. Why?"

"Pretty young for a doctorate and a teaching position in a university, don't you think? I don't know how old Caroline is, but she's a senior. She graduates in June and I've never met a more responsible, more mature student. I know she's a believer. Wasn't it your sister who had some part in that? I'd say she's one of few people I know who can give you a run for your money. I wouldn't let her go if I were you. Besides, she's a stunner!"

"You're right!" Peter said with the beginning of a grin. "I mean, I know, but I have nothing to offer her. She has a grand house and I have nothing."

"What does that have to do with it?

"I don't know. Shouldn't I have something to offer her? If I could work for a while…"

"Have you talked to her about it? Does she agree?"

"I don't know. We haven't talked about it."

"Well, maybe you should!"

"You're right, of course. It's just that I've been praying and working and waiting to get a job closer to home, and…"

"And now you have it. Well, what are you waiting for? Go fix this," Dr. Calton said with a twinkle in his eyes.

"Thank you Dr. Calton. But what if we can't get married right away? Do you think spring break would be soon enough? Or this summer?"

"I'll vouch for your character and for Caroline's. You can

be discreet on campus. If they know you're engaged, I'm sure I can reason with them."

"Thank you! Thank you!" Peter shook his hand with true gratitude.

Poor guy! He's got it bad. And no wonder! Caroline is the best thing that could have happened to him. Help him figure it out, Lord. Poor kids! Help them figure it out, Lord! And bless them!

CHAPTER TWELVE

Peter tried again. Caroline wasn't answering her phone but maybe she was driving, or maybe he had offended her so deeply that she would never talk to him again.

"Jo? Hi! I need a favor." He poured out the whole story to his sister.

"Peter! What a mess!"

"You're telling me. I need to do something for her to prove I care. Any ideas?"

"Something big?"

"Yes, really big."

"Are you going to propose?"

"Yes. Yes, I'm going to propose, nosy sister!"

"Then I have the perfect romantic way to do it."

"Spill it. Time is short."

"You're not usually so testy."

"These are uncommon times."

Jo laughed and described what she had in mind.

"Okay, but in the meantime, would you please somehow

get the message through to her that I care and I just need a little time? Tell her I'm sorry. Tell her what happened."

"Okay, big brother. Let me know what you find out. I'll be praying!"

"Thanks, Jo. Remind me later how much I owe you."

"I will!"

They were both grinning when they ended the call and went their separate ways to work out the plan. When Peter called her later, he had good news.

"They'll have it ready in three days. One day to make the drive upstate to pick it up, and they said it will take at least three days to assemble if I know what I'm doing. I'm going to get Grandpa and anyone else I can bribe to help."

"That brings us almost to Christmas Eve. That's perfect! I'll have Caroline come and stay here for a few days before Christmas."

"I'll be staying at Grandma and Grandpa's so I can work around the clock. Does she suspect anything?"

"No, Peter. You asked her to be patient and give you some time. That's what she's doing. I can hardly stand to see her so sad, Peter. I explained the terms of your contract. I don't know what she thinks, but I know it seems hopeless to her. There's something else I can't put my finger on."

"I wish she'd talk to me."

"I wish she would, too. It's not like her. There's something wrong."

"That would be me."

"I'm praying."

"Thanks, Jo."

When Jo insisted that Caroline spend some time at their house, explaining that Peter would be away, Caroline had no desire to go. If Peter returned home with a girlfriend, she did not want to be part of the welcoming party. She couldn't blame Jo for wishing Peter cared for her. All of that about his contract was a convenient way to quietly and impersonally end any expectations she may have had. Hadn't he called her Miss Engbert? That clearly laid out the new protocol. He couldn't bring someone home if she felt free to be familiar.

"I'm not taking no for an answer, Caroline," Jo stated and packed her up to take her home five days before Christmas. "We need your help. Remember how we decorated last year? Mom's counting on us and it's getting late. Jo had explained the whole plan to her mother and received permission to put off the final details of decorating as an excuse to get Caroline there.

It was hard for Caroline to feel part of the festivities. She remembered how much fun it had been last year to decorate with Jo. This year she had planned to decorate her own house, but she just hadn't felt like doing much. Maybe it was just as well to be staying at the Berkhardts' and not alone in her empty house. Empty or not, she would insist that Jo take her back home on Christmas Eve before Peter returned, and then Caroline could begin her life again, without the Berkhardts. Jo would go back to seminary and eventually away to another country. Caroline would somehow get through the next few months avoiding Peter as much as possible. She would graduate in June and then transfer to another school for her master's program. She could even live somewhere else temporarily and rent out the house until she decided if she wanted to sell it. Either renting or selling could be a good source of income, and she would be free to live wherever she chose. She could travel.

Just over a year ago, she had been so excited to return to her grandparents' home. How could she leave it now, after it had become so filled with meaning for her? If she had to leave, she would move everything personal up to her grandmother's third-story retreat and lock the door, denying access to the renters. She could never allow strangers in her grandmother's study. But how could she live, imagining Peter with someone else? *Help me, Jesus.*

Jo, Claire, Brett, Grandma Martha, and Grandpa John breathed prayers for Peter and Caroline through the days and nights. They thought of plans to distract Caroline and planned for a festive Christmas they hoped would include a very happy Peter and Caroline. Peter had given up trying to call or text Caroline. He could only pray.

To keep Caroline busy and to continue their Christmas tradition, Grandma Martha came to make Christmas cookies in her daughter's kitchen. Claire decided it was a great opportunity for the women of the family to bond even more. The kitchen was filled with the sights and smells of Christmas, and Caroline very nearly forgot her grief in the laughter and activity. Christmas carols played in the background as they baked and decorated, filling containers for Christmas day. Every few minutes, when Caroline remembered this was probably the last time she would do this with these precious women, she looked around, trying to memorize the sights and sounds and smells. Could she build these traditions for herself somewhere else, at some later time when she would feel whole again? Could she gather women around her and recreate this tradition? She couldn't imagine another family replacing this one in her heart. There was no one who could ever replace Peter in her heart. *Help me, Jesus.*

"What am I going to do, Jesus? How can I get through this?" her silent, agonized prayers continued beneath the surface current of Christmas cheer. She felt as though she might collapse at any moment.

"But those who hope in the Lord will renew their strength. They will soar on wings like eagles; they will run and not grow weary, they will walk and not be faint," the Holy Spirit whispered.

Was she just being a wimp that she couldn't stand a little rejection? Other men had rejected her. She had scorned other men. She had never minded before that a whole world full of attractive men had never come her way. Why did this have to hurt so much? Why did it matter so much that Peter had not chosen her?

"I have chosen you and have not rejected you. So do not fear, for I am with you; do not be dismayed, for I am your God. I will strengthen you and help you; I will uphold you with my righteous right hand." The words from Isaiah about how God felt about his Son applied to her as well, as a follower of that Son. How glad she was that she had memorized those verses! Whatever she had to endure, God would be with her. He had protected her and brought her back to her grandparents' home to find salvation. Her grandmother's faith was her own now and nothing could change that. That was what mattered to God and what mattered to Caroline. She could go anywhere now and know that God would not leave her. God would help her through this.

Caroline was able to smile and to keep working on Christmas cookies she had no intention of eating. They would have their Christmas celebration without her, but she had last year to remember, every precious bit of it. Someday, somewhere else she would build her own Christmas traditions. She knew she could recreate Christmas traditions anytime, anywhere, because of the spiritual heritage she had claimed. It was Christ within her who made Christmas worth celebrating. She could rejoice in that and wait on the Lord.

On Christmas Eve, Caroline couldn't persuade Jo to take her home until well past dark. How could Jo be so cheerful? Of course, Caroline hadn't told her she was not coming to Christmas dinner. She didn't want to argue about it, so she had decided she just wouldn't show up. They could do without her toffee, and she hadn't been asked to bring anything else.

"Goodbye, Jo," Caroline said, opening the car door in front of her dark house. She tried not to think of the cold empty house awaiting her lonely return.

"Oh, I'm coming with you. Grandpa says there's something in your back yard we have to see."

"Something in my back yard?"

"Yeah, come on!"

Jo hooked her arm through hers and led her around the corner of the house. She could see Christmas lights everywhere! And there, in the center of it all, just where she had always imagined it, stood a white gazebo decorated in Christmas garlands with twinkling lights and velvety bows. Her back yard was a Christmas wonder. She looked around in surprised gratitude. Such wonderful people! How could she cast them off? How could she leave them?

Movement inside the gazebo caught her eye just as she was wondering who could possibly have built the perfect gazebo in the exact spot she had chosen. She looked at Jo and back at the gazebo. Peter.

Jo gave her a gentle push toward Peter before retracing her steps and disappearing as quickly as possible. She climbed into her car and pulled away from the curb before beginning to pray in earnest.

Caroline took another step toward Peter. Peter?

"Hello, Caroline."

"Peter, did you do all of this?"

"Yes, with a little help."

"But it must have taken you days!" she blurted out a split second before realizing the conspiracy she had been part of.

"Yes, it did. I did it for you."

"But why?"

"Because I love you, Caroline."

By then, Peter had captured her hand and led her into the gazebo.

"Caroline, I'm terribly sorry about how I hurt you. I had just found out about the restrictions on faculty dating students and I didn't know what to do. I took the job because of you, Caroline. I wanted to be with you. I thought we would date and I would build up a nest egg and have *something* to offer you. You have this wonderful house and there isn't anything I can give you that you really need."

"Oh, Peter!"

"But now, I just want to be with you. Will you forgive me?"

"Of course I forgive you."

His arms were around her and Caroline felt the security of his closeness and the knowledge that he truly cared about her.

"I've been pretty miserable without you, wondering if you would ever forgive me."

"I forgive you, Peter. I've been miserable, myself. I didn't think you cared. I thought I would have to go away and try to never see you again."

He wiped the tears from her eyes. "I'm so sorry. I was here all the time, preparing this special place for you. I kept trying to tell you I loved you."

"I know. I'm sorry. I guess I just couldn't believe it."

He had dropped to one knee. "I know this is sudden, but, Caroline, will you marry me? I don't think I can ever be happy without you. There will never be anyone else. You are the one I want to spend my life with."

"Yes. Yes! But what about your job?"

"They can't object if we're married."

"They can't?"

"Of course not. Besides, I'd marry you anyway. There are other jobs. We would figure it out."

Caroline stood within the circle of his arms again. She

wanted to stay like this forever, but he interrupted her thoughts with a kiss.

"I'm sorry it took me so long to figure it out," he said with another kiss.

"Oh, Peter."

"Please don't ever go away, Caroline. I couldn't bear it."

"Never!"

"Do you think there's room for me in your grandparents' house?" Peter asked with a smile.

"More than enough room."

"In that case, I'm requesting permission to board, as soon as we're married," he said with a twinkle in his eye and another kiss.

"Permission granted."

"There is one other thing."

"What?"

"We're going to need a bigger rowboat."

Laughter filled the gazebo.

For More Information

For more information including a downloadable copy of the book of John devotional and updates about upcoming books, visit:

gailethulson.com

About the Author

Gaile Thulson holds an undergraduate degree from Wheaton College with double majors in Elementary Education and Biblical Archaeology, as well as a master's degree in Old Testament from Denver Seminary and two Master of Education degrees from the University of Northern Colorado. She loves learning and has enjoyed teaching a variety of subjects to a variety of ages in a variety of settings. Reading fiction is one of her favorite pastimes and, as a writer, she loves expressing her faith in Christ through the fiction genre, as well as nonfiction and poetry. Grateful for their spiritual heritage, she and her husband Mark enjoy passing the Christian values of their parents down to their own children and grandchildren.

Cup of Water Publishing

Giving a thirsty person a cup of water brings refreshment and can be lifesaving. Christ declared that such an action by his disciples would not go unrewarded. In the same way, giving a cup of spiritual water brings refreshment and can also be lifesaving. It is the mission of Cup of Water Publishing to give spiritual refreshment to any who are "thirsty" by making available material that is wholesome, Biblical, theologically sound, and edifying. Ultimately, our goal is to point the way to Jesus, the source of true spiritual water.

Made in the USA
Monee, IL
24 September 2022